Legends of Arcenti

Secret of the Spirits

by

Faith Landfair

Fresh Ink
an imprint of
SOCIETY OF YOUNG INKLINGS

Legends of Arcenti: Secret of the Spirits

Requests for information should be addressed to:
Society of Young Inklings, PO Box 26914, San Jose, CA 95126.

Cover Illustration: Daria Tavoularis
Interior Illustration: Faith Landfair
Interior Design and Composition: Naomi Kinsman

Printed in the USA
First Printing: February 2022
ISBN: 978-1-956380-12-5

For Jaxon.

Thank you for being an amazing brother and friend.

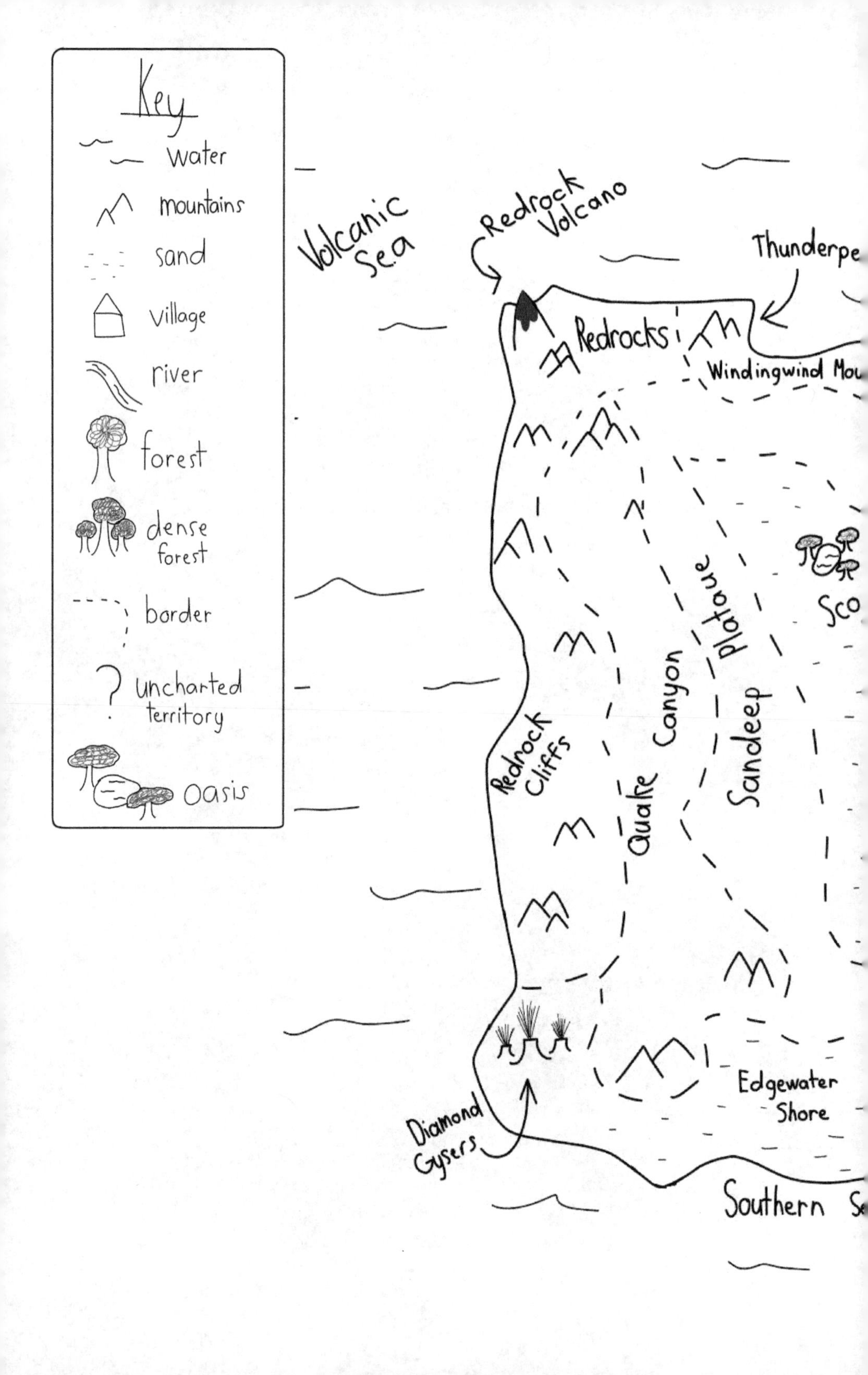
Key
water
mountains
sand
village
river
forest
dense forest
border
uncharted territory
oasis
Volcanic Sea
Redrock Volcano
Thunderpe
Redrocks
Windingwind Mou
Sco
Quake Canyon
Sandeep Platoue
Redrock Cliffs
Edgewater Shore
Diamond Gysers
Southern S

N
W
E
S

ecap
Ocean

Shadowsnow
Woods

wsand
Drop

Fang
Peak

Ancient
Ruins

Golden
Forest

Clearwater
Lake

Cascade
Valley

Clearwater
Village

Fangrocks

Silver
Forest

Synarn
Village

Lampis
Village

spire

Charponds

Aqualin
Village

Silver
Beaches

Glistening
Forest

erpent
Cove

CONTENTS

PROLOGUE

Long ago, the spirits lived in peace. They brought life to the world and everything in it. It was like this for centuries, maybe millenniums. But then, a new spirit was born. It was born out of a fight between the sky and the earth.

The spirit of darkness.

The darkness grew and fought everything in its path. To contain it, all the spirits had to combine their power and isolate it somewhere, a place out of reach and forgotten.

But the sky and earth spirits refused to let the darkness be confined to their territories, both claiming the other was to blame for the birth of darkness. They continued to fight, only letting the dark spirit grow more powerful. It began taking over other creatures, making the spirits more desperate.

Finally, the other spirits knew what they needed to do. They tore the darkness into millions of small pieces, scattering it over the world. The spirit of light came forward to help stop the darkness from spreading further. It sacrificed itself, letting the others separate it as well. For each piece of darkness, there was a piece of light.

For a while, there was peace. The spirits began preparing for a new generation of life, which they knew was coming. At last, when they were done, the world was ready for the new generation.

However, the spirits still held the memory of the dark spirit. They were afraid that, because the new creatures would be born out of light, they would also have darkness within them. So the spirits retreated to the Great Oak. They sealed themselves inside, cut off from the world, afraid to see what would come of their world with the new generations.

But the earth, sky, and water spirits refused to leave. They wanted to see what life awaited their domains, and they needed to protect that life against the darkness that was already there. It is unknown where to find them, but everything that lives can feel their presence in every breath. Every time the land shifts or the wind blows, every time a wave crashes against a beach.

CHAPTER ONE

Boreas woke up at dawn and yawned. He flicked his wings and stretched, yawning once again. Once he had blinked the sleep from his eyes, he glided down from the tree he had made his home in and into the dawning light of the Golden Forest.

The forest had been Boreas' home for his entire life. It was filled with other griffins like himself and gave him a calm, happy life. His tan fur seemed to glow with the orange light of the new day. He shook his head to clear a leaf that had been caught in his white feathers and spread his light grey wings for a moment before folding them and walking further outside.

He greeted his neighbor, a dark grey griffin with brown feathers and a black stripe down his back and tail. Blacktail waved at him and jumped atop his tree stump, which was the entrance to his home.

Everyone in the forest had a different way of making a home for themselves. Blacktail had dug out a cave underneath his tree stump. Boreas had created a shelter out of the branches of a huge tree. He also knew a family who lived by the river, their home a small mud hut nestled among the reeds growing in the water.

Boreas walked through the forest, following the path that had been made by generations of griffins walking on it and had eventually been lined with river stones to make it more visible. He reached the river and looked into the crystal clear water, watching plants rustle underneath the current. He did this every day, almost to the point where he forgot why he did it. But the truth was that he didn't want to remember why.

"Hey, Boreas!" he heard someone call.

He turned and saw Cattail trotting toward him. Cattail had dark brown fur and white feathers with a hint of blue shimmering through them. She was the daughter of Reed and Vapor, the griffins that lived by the river.

"Hey, Cattail," Boreas greeted her. "What are you up to this morning? Your parents usually don't wake up this early."

Cattail stopped at his feet and smirked. She was about as tall as his torso and thirteen years old, but she still acted like a child. Most griffins were nearly independent by the time they were ten.

"I thought I would hang around the river for a while before we went hunting," she said gleefully.

Boreas raised an eyebrow at her. "You know, if you want your mom and dad to let you have more responsibility, you should start acting more responsible."

Cattail opened her mouth to complain, but folded her wings tightly and lowered her head when she found nothing to say.

Boreas smiled at her and crouched down to look her in the eye. “You know what? I think I can help. How about you go and catch as many fish as you can, then bring them back to your parents so they don’t have to hunt today.”

Cattail tilted her head, thinking. “That’s a lot of work, though,” she complained after a moment.

Boreas stood up and shrugged. “Yeah, maybe it is, but that’s what responsibility is. If you’re not going to do it, though, I suggest heading back home before your parents wake up. Sneaking out achieves the opposite of what you want.”

Cattail sighed and thought for a while longer, then bounded away towards the best fishing spot. Boreas smiled and turned the opposite direction to continue walking down the path. He preferred other meats to fish, and he could hardly stand getting wet. He shivered at the thought of plunging into the cold water, fighting for air.

Everyone in the forest, and in Arcenti in fact, was born with a connection to one of the remaining spirits. For Boreas, it was the sky, as it was for birds and other flying creatures. Cattail and her family had a connection to the water spirit, like serpents and water-dwelling creatures. Blacktail was connected to the earth, like most land animals.

Boreas found the scent of a deer close by and followed it into the forest. Once he found it, he leapt into a tree and crouched low, waiting for the large buck to wander closer. A few moments later, the buck found itself almost directly below the tree and Boreas tackled it, killing it in one blow. He dragged it back to his home and waited below the tree for Silverpelt and Dustbeak to wake up.

It didn't take long. A sleek griffin with shiny grey fur and white feathers leapt out of the tree and smiled at Boreas. Her fur had small white speckles on it that shimmered when she moved.

Silverpelt was one of the rare creatures that was born with a connection to a different spirit than the three that stayed. Every few years, one of the hiding spirits venture out into the world to make sure they will remain safe and hidden.

On occasion, a creature would be born at the same time the spirit's energy flowed over the world, and therefore be connected to that spirit. Silverpelt was connected to the moon spirit. Whenever Boreas looked at the night sky, the luminescence reminded him of his mate.

"Morning, Silverpelt," Boreas greeted her.

He put a wing over her shoulder and she leaned against him. Her fur was as soft as silk and her feathers felt like nothing but a gentle breeze on his.

"I brought breakfast," Boreas said, flicking his long tail at the buck.

Silverpelt smiled at him and bent down to start eating.

Boreas looked back up at the tree. "Where's Dustbeak?"

Silverpelt rolled her eyes. "Who knows where that kid wandered off to."

Boreas flapped his wings to hover just below the entrance to their home and called, “Dustbeak?”

When there was no answer, Boreas sighed and landed, bending down to eat with Silverpelt. When they were done, Boreas sat up and licked the traces of meat from his beak.

“I’m going to go look for Dustbeak. He’s usually back by now,” Boreas said nervously.

“All right, but you know he’ll be fine,” Silverpelt said, beginning to sweep away the bones.

“Just in case,” Boreas reassured her. Silverpelt shrugged and Boreas trotted into the forest.

“Lost something again?” Blacktail asked jokingly as Boreas passed him.

“That kid has got to learn not to run off,” Boreas said, glancing at Blacktail.

Blacktail laughed. “Hey, at least he always comes back. *I* never did,” he offered.

Boreas sighed and jumped into the air to get a better look. He hovered above the ground and scanned the branches around him. When he didn’t see anything, he flew up through the canopy and glided over the forest. The sun was completely up now and it was casting its warm light over the trees, making the colors of the forest all the more bright. It was mid autumn and the leaves were a variety of bright oranges and reds.

Boreas spotted Dustbeak's favorite hiding spot—a huge beech tree that was struck by lightning years ago. It was hollow and had a wide trunk, making it the perfect hideout. He tucked his wings in to dive, but something shot out of the branches of the trees below him right as he started his descent, hitting him square in the chest and knocking him off balance.

"Ack! Sorry Dad!" Dustbeak called as Boreas regained his balance after falling several feet.

Boreas glared up at Dustbeak. Dustbeak had dark brown fur and tan feathers. His fur was patterned with lighter brown rings around his neck, back legs, and three on his tail. He was almost eighteen, was connected to the earth spirit, and couldn't listen to the rules to save his life.

"Where have you been?" he asked his son.

Dustbeak flicked his tail. The tuft of fur on its tip was covered in ash, and some floated off. Now that Boreas looked closer, he could see Dustbeak's paws and talons also had black smudges on them.

"Dustbeak," Boreas warned. "Where were you?'

Dustbeak lashed his tail, sending more ash floating down. "Nowhere, okay? Ashfeather and I were just hanging out."

"Ashfeather? Dustbeak, I thought we told you to stop running off with her all the time," Boreas said. He quietly added to himself, "I don't trust that girl."

"All right, all right," Dustbeak complained. "I don't need the speech again. Ashfeather is cool. I don't care whether you like her or not."

He dove into the canopy. Boreas followed him, right on his tail. He had passed his son by the time they landed in front of Silverpelt. She noticed the black marks right away.

"What is this?" she asked, grabbing Dustbeak's tail. "Were you by a fire?"

Dustbeak moaned. "I'm *fine*, Mom! It's just—we were just laying in the old beech, all right? You know it's all charred. I just got some on me, that's all."

"We?" Silverpelt echoed.

"He was hanging out with Ashfeather again," Boreas said.

Dustbeak turned and hissed, "*Dad*! It's *not* a big deal!"

"Ashfeather? Dustbeak, we talked about this! Ashfeather always seems like she's hiding something. I don't trust her, and I don't want you around her," Silverpelt stated.

Dustbeak groaned and leapt into the tree without another word.

"What are we going to do with him?" Silverpelt asked quietly, staring up at the tree.

Boreas sighed and shook his head. Dustbeak had to learn to listen to his parents, or he would get in real trouble some day.

CHAPTER TWO

The dragon was flying above the forest. It let out an ear-piercing roar and swooped down on the griffins, its huge talons outstretched and its red eyes narrowed. Dustbeak was running towards Boreas, yelling for help. But Boreas couldn't move. He couldn't do anything as the dragon soared over them and scooped up Dustbeak in its claws.

Boreas opened his eyes, shaking. *Just a dream*, he reassured himself, relaxing with the warmth of Silverpelt's fur against his. He stood and shook the clammy feeling from his wings, then peeked over Silverpelt. Dustbeak was still there, sleeping a few feet away from his parents and twitching slightly every few seconds.

Dustbeak hadn't left the house since yesterday after Boreas had found him. He had been sneaking out more frequently in the past few weeks, sometimes for entire days, but maybe the message had finally gotten through to him.

Boreas glided out of the tree and flew up to the canopy, diving under branches and dodging vines. He landed on a thick branch near the Western edge and looked out over the land beyond the forest. He had never left, though when he was younger he had dreamed about it. But it was too late now. He had a home, a family. He had a son to raise, even if that son never listened.

On this side of the forest, the land dropped into a sheer cliff and then rolled out into a vast desert. The Scorchwood Valley. The valley was surrounded by steep cliffs and treacherous mountains. It had little water and its few inhabitants fought every day to survive. There were only two oases in sight of the forest, one of which was directly below the cliffs. Sometimes griffins went there to collect fireflowers.

Each oasis was surrounded by scorchwood trees, one of the most dangerous plants known to the griffins. The trees' sap was poisonous, even to touch, and their leaves were so easily flammable that a hot breeze could make them start to smoke. The trees' bark was also very flammable and produced tiny splinters that were near impossible to get out. The one good thing about the trees was that they grew fireflowers, sweet-smelling flowers that produced nectar that helped heal all kinds of wounds.

Boreas had heard tales of elves living within the few oases that could be found in the desert, eating anything they could find... including griffins.

That was how the stories went, anyway. Boreas didn't think that was true, though he did fear elves just as any other griffin would. A griffin unlucky enough to encounter an elf community was unlikely to survive. The elves hated griffins and would kill one on sight. Boreas's grandfather had tried to instil a deep fear in his family by telling them he lost his talon to the elves, though Boreas had always suspected he had lost it to something else. Boreas didn't really believe that the elves could be so vicious, especially if they were intelligent enough to make whole villages and even speak the same language, though few griffins had the chance to make conversation with them.

While he watched the sunlight fill the valley, he heard wingbeats behind him. Boreas swerved his head around to see where the noise was coming from and saw the trees shaking slightly. The sound was getting louder. Boreas suddenly felt a gust of wind and crouched down, digging his claws into the tree to prevent himself from falling.

Above him, a huge creature with giant leather wings and talons the size of Boreas's head flew over. It had thick green scales and long blue spines.

A dragon! Boreas realized with alarm. *What is a dragon doing this far away from the Fangrocks?* He remembered his dream and crouched lower.

He watched, frozen in fear, as the dragon tilted its wings and started descending toward the Scorchwood Valley. It landed at the base of the cliff and stalked toward the oasis. It stopped, almost as tall as the scorchwoods, and bent down to lap up water from the small pond. Boreas took this as a chance to creep backwards into the foliage, hidden from the dragon. He turned and fled into the protection of the forest, not stopping until he reached his home and bumped into Silverpelt.

"Boreas, are you all right?" she asked.

"Did you see that?" someone called from behind him. There were griffins gathering in the clearing.

"A dragon!" another griffin yelled.

"Here? In the Golden Forest?" someone else chimed in.

"I saw it!"

"Why did it leave the Fangrocks?"

"What is it doing here?"

"Did it come for the forest?"

"Where did it go?"

"I saw it land in the Scorchwood Valley," Boreas said over the noise. Everyone turned to him and immediately started asking questions.

"It came from the East, as far as I could see," Boreas said, trying to answer all the questions. "I didn't stick around to find out if it left or not. No, it didn't see me. It landed next to the oasis."

"Everyone calm down!" Silverpelt yelled. The murmurs slowed to a stop.

"We need to figure this out and make sure it didn't hurt anyone. Does anyone know if there are griffins at the oasis this morning?" Silverpelt asked.

After a bit more chatter, someone spoke up. "Bronzefeather left before the sun rose to gather fireflowers!"

"Did he come back? Does anyone see him? Bronzefeather!" Silverpelt called.

After a few minutes of more talking and yelling, they couldn't find Bronzefeather.

"We have to go look for him!" Blacktail insisted.

"But the dragon might still be there!" Vapor argued.

"But he might need help!" another griffin said.

"I'll go!" Dustbeak announced from the tree.

Everyone looked up at him and the yelling started again.

"He'll save Bronzefeather!"

"It's too dangerous!"

"Boreas, doesn't your son know about dragons?"

"He's a hero!"

"Everyone quiet!" Silverpelt finally yelled, silencing the crowd.

Boreas turned to Dustbeak as Silverpelt tried to keep the arguments at bay. "What are you thinking?" he asked, narrowing his eyes.

"Ashfeather lives around there. She'll know if the dragon is gone, and we can fly down there and save Bronzefeather!" Dustbeak declared.

"And what if the dragon is still there? Or she says it's gone but it's not?" Boreas asked.

"We'll see it. Dragons are *huge*. It can't hide in an oasis," Dustbeak scoffed.

"It can if it's below the scorchwood trees. Look, even if the dragon *did* leave, does your master plan involve getting poisoned with scorchwood sap? Or stabbed with splinters? What if the trees are on fire?" Boreas pointed out.

Dustbeak flared his wings. "We'll be *fine*, dad!"

Before Boreas could stop him, Dustbeak flapped his tan wings and soared over the crowd, disappearing above the canopy.

"Dustbeak!" Silverpelt cried.

Boreas didn't hesitate in jumping into the air and following his son. When he caught up to him, Dustbeak was landing on the ground, only a few feet away from the cliff. He walked towards a redwood tree and looked up into it, calling Ashfeather's name.

The small griffin glided down from the tree only a few seconds after. Her fur was white and her feathers were dark grey and faded into white near the tips of her wings, and there were white circles around her eyes. Her beak was an unusually light golden-brown color.

"Ashfeather, did you see that dragon that landed in the desert?" Dustbeak asked after a brief greeting.

Ashfeather nodded, ignoring Boreas as he landed behind Dustbeak.

"Is it gone?" Dustbeak asked.

Ashfeather nodded again. "It flew away a few minutes ago, towards the northern cliffs. I thought the whole oasis was going to burn down, but the trees seemed to have stopped smoking now."

Dustbeak turned toward the valley and started opening his wings. "Come on. Bronzefeather went down there this morning and didn't come back. We have to make sure he's all right."

Ashfeather followed him and the three of them glided down to the oasis. They landed just outside the scorchwood trees and started walking cautiously towards the water.

"Be careful," Boreas said.

Dustbeak shot him a resentful look but said nothing as they wandered deeper into the trees. Boreas felt splinters pricking his feet and tried to avoid touching the tree trunks.

Finally, they made it to the water. The area was filled with smoke from the leaves and there were talon prints twice the size of the griffins' prints. Boreas stepped in one and almost tripped as his talon got stuck in the mud. He pulled it out and kept walking.

"Bronzefeather?" Dustbeak called.

"Hello? Is someone there?" a voice asked from above them.

They looked up and saw a large golden-brown griffin with rust colored feathers sitting in the treetops. His tail was curled tightly around the branch and there were scratches in the bark where he had been holding. Boreas noticed a sack of fireflowers discarded on the ground below the tree.

"It's okay, the dragon's gone," Ashfeather reassured him.

Bronzefeather slowly loosened his grip and spread his wings to glide down to them.

"Are you all right?" Boreas asked when he landed.

Bronzefeather let out a shaky breath and said, "Yeah, I'm fine. Just spooked. I thought it saw me fly into the tree, but then it left."

"It's okay, you're safe now. Let's get you back to the forest," Dustbeak said.

They started walking away from the oasis, the trees being too thick to fly through without the risk of touching the sap. Once they made it out they spread their wings to fly, but a voice stopped them.

"So there *was* someone in the trees. I thought I saw something when we flew in."

They whirled around and saw an elf, about as tall as Boreas, leaning against a tree. Her skin was light grey and she was wearing a brown tunic. She had short, dark red hair tucked behind her pointed ears and slung over her shoulder was a leather bag.

All the stories of elves came back to Boreas and he wanted to fly away as fast as he could. *What if they're true? They could be entirely true! We could die!*

"Don't worry, I'm not here to hurt you," the elf said impatiently. "I just want to talk."

"I think we'll be heading home," Dustbeak said slowly, taking a few steps back.

The elf shrugged. "All right, then. I guess you can talk to my friend."

Ashfeather screamed. Boreas saw that she had turned around, and he turned to see what she was screaming at.

Behind them was the dragon, a little over twice as tall as them and only a few steps away, growling. Its bright yellow-green eyes were staring straight at them.

The others saw the dragon as well and backed away from it, almost running into the elf.

"Change your mind?" the elf asked, smirking and placing a hand on her hip.

"What do you want?" Boreas asked, spreading his wings in front Dustbeak.

The elf leaned forward. "Like I said, I just want to talk."

"And feed us to your dragon when you're done? No thanks," Ashfeather spat.

The elf raised an eyebrow and said, "Yeah, no. I'm not interested in killing anyone. *But* I do recommend coming with me, unless you want me to find someone more willing in the forest. I think that would cause a lot more trouble don't you? But I saw a moon griffin in there that might help."

Boreas lashed his tail and crouched, hissing, "If you go anywhere near Silverpelt, I will—"

The elf interrupted him. "So we have a deal then! Great. Let's go." She waved her hand at them and took a step.

"Whoa, whoa, whoa, I'm not going anywhere," Bronzefeather said, planting his feet into the ground.

Boreas saw his wings twitch anxiously and guessed every sense was entirely aware of the dragon behind them, but he was doing a good job at acting fierce despite that.

"All right, fine. I don't need someone who's afraid of dragons. Go home and make sure everyone knows you're fine and your friends are fine. Go on," the elf insisted.

Bronzefeather backed up cautiously and turned around, spreading his wings. He lifted high into the air and flapped away. The dragon lifted its head and snorted at him, making him falter for a moment before regaining his balance. Bronzefeather looked back at them before he entered the trees, then he was gone.

Boreas turned back to the elf, his fur prickling as he felt the dragon's breath on his neck.

"Follow me," the elf said.

"Why?" Ashfeather asked. "What do you want to 'talk' about? Why do you need us?"

The elf looked at Ashfeather and narrowed her eyes. "I said follow me. I'll explain everything once we're off the sand."

"No!" Ashfeather cried.

Dustbeak put a talon on her shoulder and looked at her.

Ashfeather shook her head. "I—I can't go with you!"

"Hey, if you want to leave, go ahead," the elf said. "But the other two stay."

"I'm not leaving without Dustbeak," Ashfeather insisted, lifting her chin.

"Then let's go," the elf spat.

Ashfeather stayed where she was.

The elf crossed her arms and narrowed her eyes, but then her look softened. "Just go," the elf said.

Boreas looked at Ashfeather, then back at the elf, but he couldn't read their faces.

"Go," Dustbeak whispered to her. "I'll be all right."

"I'm not leaving you," Ashfeather said.

"I'll be fine. Tell my mom what happened. I'll be back as soon as I can," Dustbeak said firmly.

Ashfeather spread her wings hesitantly.

"Ashfeather, just go," Boreas said.

"We'll be fine," Dustbeak insisted again.

Ashfeather laid her head against his, then flew into the air. She dove towards the forest, staring back at them until she reached the cliff.

"And now there's two," the elf said. Her voice was almost cheerful and had a hint of humor in it. "And I'm not letting you two go. Come on. Can we please get out of here before the sun gets too high?"

Boreas shifted his feet and looked around nervously. In the middle of the day, the sand got hot enough to burn anything it touched. As if that wasn't bad enough, that was when the sandents came out to hunt, burrowing through the ground and sneaking up on anyone with ease. Thinking of the snake-like predators, Boreas suddenly would rather do anything but stay out in the open like this.

The two of them reluctantly followed the elf towards her dragon. The huge beast stood and fell in line behind them as they entered a cave in the cliff. They sat down inside the cave and the elf set a few twigs on the ground. Boreas didn't pay attention as she lit the fire; he was watching the dragon settle in behind her.

"By the way, my name is Mira," the elf said as she stacked more twigs onto the fire. "What are your names?"

"I'm Dustbeak," Dustbeak said cautiously. "This is my father, Boreas."

"Nice to meet you," Mira said. When the fire got large enough to light the cave, she asked, "I assume you know our world's history?"

"Of course," Dustbeak scoffed. "Now why did you bring us here?"

"So you know of the spirits," she said, ignoring Dustbeak's question.

"Yes," Boreas said. "Who wouldn't?"

"The spirits are beginning to grow restless. It started slowly—stronger rains, a few earthquakes, things like that. But it's beginning to get more noticeable. We think they're trying to warn us about something," Mira explained.

"What?" Boreas asked, suddenly interested.

"The darkness," Mira said.

She reached her hand toward the fire. Suddenly, the flames were so big they brushed against the ceiling. Boreas scooted away until his back was against the wall. Mira fisted her hand and the fire curled around itself, forming into a ball.

"What in the world..." Dustbeak breathed, backing up to sit next to Boreas.

Boreas smiled to himself for a moment. Dustbeak never got this close to him anymore, even when he was scared. It was nice to know his son still depended on him.

"Thousands of years ago, the spirits banished the darkness by tearing it apart and scattering it over the world. And the light followed to keep it from growing stronger," Mira started. "Everyone knows this. But what they don't know is that when the new generation came, it wasn't born out of nothing. It was made from the dark and light. These spirits are not in certain places, locked away like some believe. They are within every one of us. But the darkness is growing, and in some it has taken over completely and chased the light away."

"But why now? And what does this have to do with us?" Boreas asked.

Mira looked up at him and lowered her hand, letting the fire return to normal. "I believe that we can stop it. If we can find the other spirits, they can still save the light. The darkness has grown steadily over time, and it will only get stronger if we don't do something."

"Why us?" Dustbeak asked.

"Well, you're the first griffins I've been able to corner, and there were only two other elves I know that would be helpful, and they're both too old. My theory is that it will be easier to find the spirits if we have more of a connection to them. I was looking specifically for someone like me, someone who's connected to a spirit that's in hiding. I was hoping maybe you two could lead me to one." She glanced at Boreas and added in a softer voice, "I know the moon griffin I saw means a lot to you. It doesn't have to be her. But is there another? Someone who has a deep connection to the spirits?"

Boreas thought for a moment. Then he realized what the elf had said. "Someone like you?"

Mira nodded. She opened her palm and reached toward the fire again. The fire twisted and a piece of it flew towards her and landed just above her hand. She lifted it closer to her, then closed her fist. The fire vanished.

"The fire spirit," Dustbeak realized.

"How did you..." Boreas trailed off. He had never seen anything like this before. Maybe elves had powers depending on what spirit they were connected to?

"You can do it too," Mira said, smiling at them. "Not with fire, but you have more relation with the spirits than you realize. Everyone does."

Dustbeak went silent and looked at his feet, his wings twitching thoughtfully.

Boreas thought for a moment. He couldn't put Silverpelt in danger. Who else would be willing to help? He could only think of one other griffin in the forest that was different—Brightwing. He was one of the older griffins, so maybe he would understand. Though he did have a reputation for being stubborn.

"There's one other," Boreas said slowly. "Brightwing. He has the sun spirit."

"Perfect," Mira said. "Let's go get him."

Boreas hesitated. He was about to bring an elf and a dragon into his home and convince Brightwing that he could save the world. It was a crazy plan, and they had almost no reason to trust Mira.

But somehow, Boreas felt that Mira was telling the truth. They needed to do something, and Brightwing might be the only one who could help them.

CHAPTER THREE

"What!"

Boreas winced. Brightwing apparently found leaving the Golden Forest an unthinkable concept. And Boreas hadn't even mentioned Mira yet.

"What could possibly be out there to make leaving worth it?" Brightwing asked.

Boreas had asked Brightwing if he had ever wanted to leave the forest. When the answer was a definite no, he tried to tell Brightwing that it would be worth it. Clearly that wasn't working.

Brightwing folded his wings and sat down, his black fur shimmering in the late sunlight. His feathers were almost the same bright orange as the leaves above them, which were blowing in the wind that had picked up on their way to Brightwing's home. Mira and her dragon were waiting just outside the forest, out of view from the already terrified population of griffins. She had Dustbeak with her—Boreas suspected that was a kind of threat to make sure he came back.

"Maybe it's not as dangerous as everyone says," Boreas offered.

Brightwing scoffed. "Yeah, generations of griffins were actually lying about the perils outside of the forest and stayed here for absolutely no reason. Sounds about right. Why do you even want me to go with you?"

Boreas sighed. "Okay, the truth is that something is happening. The spirits are angry, and I think we need to do something about it."

"So why me? There are dozens of other griffins in this forest. And frankly, most of them are much younger than me," Brightwing said.

"Because we need to find the hiding spirits, and you're connected to one of them," Boreas explained.

"There are others," Brightwing said flatly. "Isn't your mate one of them? How come you're not risking *her* life instead of mine?"

Boreas was about to argue, but a strong gust of wind swept over them. He looked at the sky and saw a blanket of dark clouds threatening to pour rain on them.

Brightwing saw the clouds as well and looked back at his house, which was a dome-shaped nest woven from branches and leaves with a large hole in the wall for an entrance.

"Maybe we should go inside," he said. "It looks like a pretty bad storm. Water makes my bones ache."

Boreas watched the trees above them shake violently in the wind and felt the first few drops of rain on his head. He heard thunder in the distance and looked to Brightwing, who was starting to back towards his nest.

"I don't know if those thin leaves are going to keep us dry," Boreas said, nodding at the roof of the dome.

"My home is perfectly fine. It might be a little rickety, but it keeps me out of the weather," Brightwing said defensively. "But *you* are *entirely* welcome to go back to your *own* home."

Boreas shook his head and took a step towards Brightwing, debating whether he should keep trying or not. Then the wind got stronger and the entire top of Brightwing's nest flew away in it. Brightwing watched it go and cursed under his breath.

"Don't you see?" Boreas yelled over the wind and rain. "This is exactly why we need to go! The Golden Forest never used to get storms like this!"

"It's just a storm!" Brightwing argued. "We've had plenty of storms in the past. This one is no different! The spirits aren't angry at us!"

Just then, there was a bright flash of light followed by a loud bang. Boreas crouched and waited for his ears to stop ringing and his eyes to work again. When he could see, he noticed a tree not too far away in flames. He looked at Brightwing and lifted an eyebrow.

Brightwing glared back and growled, "that doesn't prove anything!"

"Do you want to get out of this rain or not?" Boreas asked.

Brightwing glowered at Boreas for a few seconds. Then, hearing another clap of thunder, he lashed his tail and walked over to Boreas.

Boreas turned and said, “Follow me,” then started running towards the Northern edge of the forest.

“I thought you lived near the Western end,” Brightwing called.

“We’re not going to my house,” Boreas responded.

They ran until they reached the North Mountain, which marked the border of the forest. Boreas led Brightwing into an open cave in the side of the mountain, seeing the flickering glow of firelight from inside.

When they entered, Boreas rushed ahead and told Mira and Dustbeak to hide deeper in the cave. He needed more time with Brightwing before introducing the elf.

“Why here?” Brightwing asked once they had sat by the fire.

“Oh, uh, Silverpelt was doing some upgrades on the house and I don’t think she was finished, so it wouldn’t be much better than yours.”

Brightwing gave him a suspicious look. “Are you going to keep trying to get me to go with you? Because if that’s why you brought me here, the answer is still no.”

“Brightwing, would you just look outside? This never happens!” Boreas exclaimed.

“Boreas, for the last time, I don’t want to leave the forest on some pretend mission and risk my life for nothing!” Brightwing yelled.

He turned his back to Boreas and laid down next to the fire. "I'm leaving as soon as the storm dies down, end of story."

Boreas sighed and stood up to walk further into the cave to find Mira. He hadn't wanted to force Brightwing the same way Mira forced them to listen to her, but that could be the only way.

"Boreas, that you?" Mira's voice whispered.

Boreas squinted into the dark and saw her and Dustbeak sitting next to each other, the dragon sleeping behind them.

"It's me," Boreas answered. "But it's not good news."

"Do you want me to send Nightshade out?" Mira asked. Her dragon lifted its head and blinked, its eyes glowing in the dark.

"It has a name?" Boreas asked, surprised.

Mira narrowed her eyes. "Of course she does. We all have names, don't we? Dragons are the same as us."

"But they don't seem, I mean, they aren't..." Boreas trailed off.

"Intelligent?" Mira asked. "Dragons aren't intelligent? Is that what you're saying?"

"No, I just—"

"Guys, we're wasting time," Dustbeak cut in, saving Boreas unintentionally. "If Brightwing won't help us, we have to get my mom. They're the only griffins we know that could help."

"We're not endangering Silverpelt," Boreas stated. He turned to Mira. "Do what you have to do."

Mira stood and held up two fingers, waving them toward the entrance. Nightshade stood up and started walking slowly.

Mira followed her and Boreas watched them go, not wanting to see Brightwing get scared out of his wits. Dustbeak looked at him, then followed Mira.

A few seconds later Boreas heard Brightwing yell in alarm, followed by a long argument between the three of them. Near the end of the conversation they fell silent and Boreas saw the light from the fire seem to grow, then die down.

Finally he heard Brightwing say, “Fine. I’ll go.”

Boreas turned around and joined them in the firelight, and Brightwing gave him a betrayed look.

“I’m sorry,” Boreas pleaded. “I didn’t want to force you, but...”

Brightwing looked away. The rain had slowed down and the wind had all but stopped, so they went outside.

“So where do we go?” Dustbeak asked. “Do we have any idea where they are?”

“According to legend, the spirits rest in the Great Oak,” Mira said.

“Which is where?” Dustbeak prompted.

Mira tilted her head back and forth. “Well, no one really knows. That’s kind of the point of hiding in it—no one knows where it is. But that’s why we need Brightwing. With enough connection to the spirits, the two of us might be able to communicate with them. Or at least get some sense of where they are.”

“Great,” Brightwing said. “So we have no clue how or where to find them and only a theory on why we’re even doing this.”

Boreas frowned. That was pretty accurate. He still didn't know why he was going along with Mira, and he expected Brightwing to blindly follow. Why?

Mira pulled out a large rolled up piece of paper from her bag and spread it out on the ground in front of her.

"What is this?" Boreas asked, touching the paper lightly with his claw.

It felt smooth and thin, not like he expected something made from a tree would feel. He had heard of elves making paper out of trees and writing on them, but this had multiple colors and different shapes all over the parchment.

"You've never seen a map before?" Mira asked.

The three griffins shook their heads.

"Wow, the Golden Forest really is cut off from the world."

The elf tapped a spot on the middle of the paper, which was a green and brown patch with a black squiggly line in the center. Boreas noticed different lines like this one scattered over the map, each one in a slightly different pattern and located on different patches.

"This is the Golden Forest," Mira said. She pointed to a larger patch of dark yellow with a few tiny green spots inside it, just to the left of the forest. "And this is the Scorchwood Valley. All the places in Arcenti are shown on this map, see?"

Boreas looked at the different places on the map. He noticed a small black circle with four lines in it on one of the corners. Next to each line was another scribble. "What's that place?" he asked, pointing to it.

"That's the compass. It tells you which direction on the map is North, East, South, and West. See how the W points to the West side? And the N to the North?"

Boreas tilted his head and Brightwing asked, "What?"

"Oh boy, you guys can't read either," Mira said, touching her hand to her forehead. "Okay, so these are letters, and letters make up words. Like this says Golden Forest." She pointed to the small squiggle in the middle of the green patch.

"What's this place?" Dustbeak asked, pointing to the top of the map.

There was a big blue patch with small white dots that took up most of the space at the top.

"That's the Icecap Ocean," Mira said. "And the Volcanic Sea is here."

She pointed to a darker blue spot in the top left corner.

"And this?" Brightwing tapped a long grey stripe along the right side of the map.

"The Fangrocks," Mira said. "That's where most dragons live."

"Where do you live?" Dustbeak asked.

Mira leaned over the map and pointed to a lighter green area below the Golden Forest. "The Silver Forest is where I was raised, but Nightshade and I don't really have a specific place to call home."

"Why are you showing us this?" Boreas asked.

"Right, I was going to show you the paths we could take. There are a few probable theories as to where the Great Oak could be, and I thought we could start there. Besides, if we get close to it I think we'll be able to feel them. The first one is here, in the Golden Forest. That's why I'm here. But clearly it's not here, or you would know. Another theory is that it could be at the Charponds, over here," Mira explained.

She pointed to dark blue, almost purple smudges to the right of the Fangrocks.

"Some also say it's located on top of the Skyspire, which is the tallest mountain in Arcenti. It's on the border of the Silver Forest and the Scorchwood Valley," Mira said.

She tapped a light grey spot to the left and slightly below the Silver Forest.

"The last option is Quake Canyon, right there." Mira pointed to a long strip of dark brown on the left side of the map.

"They all sound pretty far away," Brightwing said skeptically.

"Which is the most likely option?" Boreas asked. "I don't want to fly all that way for no reason."

Mira shrugged. "These three are the most likely of all the theories. I've been collecting information and narrowing it down for years. The truth is, I've already been near most of these places. But never with the intent of finding the Great Oak, and only with Nightshade. I think having someone else who's connected to the hiding spirits might be the key."

"The Skyspire seems like the closest, but I don't know if I would be able to fly to the top. Wouldn't the air get too thin for us anyway?" Dustbeak pointed out.

"And we definitely don't want to go to the Charponds. We'd have to cross through the Fangrocks," Brightwing said.

"Or go around them, through the Glistening Forest," Mira suggested, tracing her finger down the grey stripe and through a light green splotch below it. "But that's probably twice as dangerous."

"What about Quake Canyon?" Boreas suggested. "It seems easier to reach."

"If you want to cross the Scorchwood Valley," Dustbeak said. "Unless we avoid it by following this stretch of brown."

He pointed to a light brown streak above the Scorchwood Valley that ended in a large square next to Quake Canyon.

"The Sandeep Plateau isn't much better than the valley," Mira said. "It's just miles and miles of flat rock. We'd be better off going through the desert. At least then we have oases."

"I think the Skyspire is the closest and easiest to get to," Brightwing said. "Even if the air does get thin, at least we won't have to deal with dragons or lifeless deserts."

"Sounds all right with me," Boreas said.

He didn't love the idea of barely being able to breathe, but it was better than the other two options.

But why am I going along with this in the first place?

"All right, we're going to the Skyspire then," Mira said.

She rolled up her map and placed it back into her sack. "It's getting late. We'll leave in the morning. Meet me here at sunrise."

Boreas and Dustbeak nodded. Boreas couldn't believe she was trusting them to return, and it was even more baffling to know he was going to.

But Brightwing hesitated. "What makes you think I'll come?"

Mira looked at him. "I have a feeling you want to save the world just as much as we do."

Brightwing stared at her for a long time and flexed his talons. Finally he nodded and turned around to fly back to the forest. The clouds had cleared and they could see the sun starting to set over the forest as he flew away.

Mira nodded to them and Boreas and Dustbeak set off towards home. When they arrived, they found Silverpelt sleeping below the tree and Ashfeather pacing around the clearing. As soon as she saw them she sprinted over and wrapped her wings around Dustbeak, then nodded respectfully to Boreas.

"Are you all right? What happened? Where's the elf?" Ashfeather asked quickly.

"We're fine," Dustbeak said. "But we're going back tomorrow."

"Why?" Ashfeather asked, her eyes wide. "Did she threaten you? Is the dragon going to hurt you? I shouldn't have left, I'm so sorry, I—"

"Ash, we're fine!" Dustbeak put his wing on the side of her face and made her look at him. "The elf is on our side. She's not going to hurt us, and neither is her dragon."

Ashfeather sighed and leaned into him. "Why do you have to go then?"

Dustbeak looked down at her and said, "We have to help the spirits."

Ashfeather looked up at him and fell silent. Boreas saw some kind of understanding pass between them, like a secret they had hinted at but had not said aloud.

Boreas also saw something he hadn't accepted before. They cared for each other. He thought he was being a good father trying to keep them away from each other. But even if he didn't trust Ashfeather, they needed each other. Boreas didn't know what he would have done if someone had tried to keep him away from Silverpelt.

He decided not to wake Silverpelt because she looked as if she had spent all day pacing the clearing, so he laid down beside her and blanketed her with his wing. Boreas watched Dustbeak and Ashfeather talk for a while longer, then go into the tree to sleep. For a moment he wondered if he should go up there and keep an eye on them, but he knew they would be fine. Dustbeak was almost eighteen now. He could handle the night alone. For the first time, he didn't worry about what his son was doing. He could just lie here with Silverpelt.

A thought crossed his mind just before he fell asleep, and it made him uneasy.

This could be the last night he spent in the Golden Forest.

CHAPTER FOUR

The wind swept under Boreas's wings as he lifted into the air next to Dustbeak. There was a small light to their left, coming from the sun that was not yet above the horizon. The moon was just setting and the stars were beginning to disappear.

Boreas looked down on the Golden Forest, where Silverpelt and Ashfeather were watching them leave. Silverpelt had been overjoyed to wake up and find Boreas beside her, but her happiness was dulled when he told her he had to leave again. She understood, though, and didn't argue.

Mira was behind them, riding Nightshade. Boreas's fur still prickled when he got too close to the dragon. But he tilted his wing and glided to the side of them to look at the strange piece of leather on Nightshade's back. Mira had buckled it onto the dragon just before they took off, and now she was sitting on top of it. She called it a 'saddle', but Boreas had no clue what it was for.

Brightwing glided underneath them, still refusing to talk to Boreas. Apparently he was still mad at Boreas for tricking him, which Boreas understood.

"We'll reach the Southern border by midday at the latest," Mira called. "Then we'll follow the edge of the Silver Forest until we reach the Skyspire."

"Um, isn't the Silver Forest crawling with elves?" Brightwing asked.

And isn't the Golden Forest crawling with griffins?" Mira retorted. "We fear you just as much as you fear us. All the stories you hear are just superstitions. We have the same ones, but with the roles reversed."

"But I personally know griffins who have been hurt by elves," Dustbeak argued.

"And I personally know elves who have been hurt by griffins," Mira snapped.

The griffins fell silent. For a while the only thing they heard was the wind and Nightshade's heavy breathing, along with her wingbeats.

"Here we are," Mira said eventually.

Boreas squinted. "I don't see the end of the forest," he said.

"That's because there is no end, not until the Silver Beaches. The Golden and Silver forests aren't separate. They're just divided into two sections. During the Spirit's Era, before elves and griffins parted ways, it was called the Emerald Woodland," Mira explained.

"I see the Skyspire!" Brightwing exclaimed.

Boreas followed his gaze to their right and saw a huge mountain, the peak reaching higher than the clouds. It was on the other side of the Silver Forest, on the border of the Scorchwood Valley.

They folded their wings and dove towards the ground, landing on the edge of the forest. Boreas shook his wings out and looked around nervously. He had never left his home before.

"These old wings aren't as strong as they used to be," he heard Brightwing mutter.

"We'll walk for a while. Rest your wings. You'll need all your energy to fly up the spire," Mira said.

They started walking in silence, leaving deep footprints in the soft dirt. Boreas's senses were alert in this strange place. Every time a twig snapped or the trees rustled he jumped and scanned the area for elves. At one point, a falcon got spooked by Nightshade and flapped itself right into Boreas, scaring both of them and making Mira laugh at him. The entire time Boreas was sure to stay close to Dustbeak.

After almost an hour of walking, Boreas heard rustling in the trees that sounded too heavy to be birds. He looked around for any sign of what had made the noise, but there was nothing in sight and the forest was silent again.

"Did you guys hear that?" Boreas asked the others.

Mira rolled her eyes. "It was just a bird, Boreas. Just like the last fifteen sounds you've asked me about."

"I don't know, this one sounded different," Dustbeak said.

"What if we're being followed?" Brightwing asked.

“Who would be following us?” Mira asked, irritated.

“What if it’s elves?” Boreas worried. “Don’t elves live in the Silver Forest? They could be stalking us.”

“If we are being followed by elves, it’s because they’re curious. They’ll be too scared of you three to get too close, though,” Mira said. “Come on, we need to hurry if we want to reach the Skyspire by morning.”

They continued walking, hearing more noise every few minutes. Boreas looked up between the trees and saw the sky beginning to darken, making him even more nervous. It bothered him that Mira seemed to not notice the sounds at all. Once the sun had set, they stopped to rest and Mira made a small fire.

Boreas looked into the fire and thought about everything that had happened in the past few days. He had encountered an elf and a dragon, and now they were in a strange land with the threat of being stalked by foreign inhabitants. He got up and paced, thinking that maybe he could just fly away right now. But what would happen if he did? Looking up at the stars, he thought of Silverpelt.

What in the world have I decided to do?

That night he slept uneasily, his back to the fire. In the morning, they got up early and continued their trek towards the mountain.

They were almost to the edge of the forest when he heard loud footsteps behind them. The four of them turned around but saw no one.

"Hello?" Mira called.

It was quiet for a few seconds. Then, a small voice came from the trees.

"Mira?"

Mira faced the voice and looked into the canopy. Boreas squinted and saw a dark shape crouched in the tree. He took a step back and pointed the figure out to Dustbeak and Brightwing.

Mira walked closer to the elf in the tree and called up, "Who's there?"

The elf leaned further out and whispered a name that Boreas couldn't hear. When Mira heard it her eyes softened and she smiled. The small elf started climbing down the tree but stopped in the lower branches.

"Mira, there are griffins behind you!" she cried.

"It's all right, Keko. They're friends," Mira said gently.

The little elf's eyes went wide. "You made friends with *griffins*?" she asked, astonished.

Mira nodded and gestured for Keko to climb down. She jumped onto the ground and wrapped her arms around Mira. She was only as tall as her waist and had the same grey skin as Mira, only slightly brighter and her hair was black.

Once they were done hugging, Mira introduced Keko to the griffins.

"Keko, this is Boreas, Dustbeak, and Brightwing," she said, gesturing to the three of them in turn. "And this is my little sister, Keko," she finished, patting Keko on the back.

Boreas said nothing. One elf and a dragon was frightening enough for him, but another elf? And this must be a very young elf to be so small, which means there had to be more around.

"Mira," Brightwing said. His voice was slightly strained, as if he was trying not to yell. "I think we should be going soon. We won't be able to reach the Skyspire before midday if we don't leave right now."

Mira sighed and crouched down so she was face-to-face with Keko. "Keko, I have to leave again. But I promise I'll come back as soon as I can, okay?"

Keko looked at the griffins and asked quietly, "Are they making you go? I can fight them! Uh, well, maybe not me. I can go get help! Don't worry, Mira, stay here and we'll save you in no time!"

Mira laughed and put her hand on Keko's cheek. "No, Keko. I have a dragon, remember? Nobody can boss me around. In fact, I'm the one in charge of them right now."

Keko looked back at the griffins, then to her sister. Boreas watched curiously. This didn't seem like the child of bloodthirsty beasts that ripped griffins apart with ease, like the stories told. This was just a little kid that was worried for her sister.

Maybe we were wrong about more than I thought.

"Hey, it'll be all right," Mira reassured her sister. "I'll be back before you know it."

Keko looked into Mira's eyes and smiled. She hugged her sister once more, then ran over to Nightshade and put a hand on her shoulder. The dragon lowered her head and made a soft growling sound.

Then the small elf ran back into the woods, yelling, "Mom! Dad! You won't believe it!"

Mira stood up and turned to keep walking without saying a word to the griffins.

Boreas and the others followed her silently, exchanging glances. A bird flew overhead, but Boreas was too focused on Mira to look up at it. They still had a few hours until they would reach the Skyspire, so he decided to spend them figuring out Mira. She seemed so fierce and strong, but now she just looked... sad.

They arrived at the base of the Skyspire a little after midday. The sun was resting right above the mountain, blinding Boreas whenever he tried to look up at the spire.

"It's at the top of that?" Dustbeak said weakly.

"Tip top," Mira said, climbing onto Nightshade.

"It's so tall..." Brightwing said.

"And it's not getting any shorter with you staring at it," Mira pointed out. "Let's go."

Boreas spread his wings and followed Nightshade into the air, climbing higher by the second. The mountain seemed endless and the sun was blinding. After almost two hours of flying in silence, Boreas saw Nightshade tilt her wings and level off, soaring into a small divot in the mountain. It was deep enough to create a landing space large enough for them to stand squeezed together.

"We'll stop every chance we get to rest," Mira said. "Near the top there will be less spots like this one."

"How tall is this thing?" Dustbeak asked, out of breath. "We're as high as the clouds and I still can't see the top."

"It's up there," was all Mira said.

Once they had caught their breath they took off again, though Boreas's wings complained as he spread them. He had never flown for hours at a time before this, and he admitted to himself that he was slightly out of shape. They stopped two more times, each time the ledge was further away from the last.

On the third ledge, Boreas found it even harder to catch his breath. He peeked over the edge and immediately felt like he was going to topple over. The ground was so far away he could barely make out the trees from the grass.

"Oh ya, I don't suggest looking down," Mira said. She sounded just as breathless as the rest of them, even though she hadn't been flying.

"The air is getting thin," Dustbeak wheezed. "Are we almost to the top?"

"I think we can make it if we fly for a little under a half hour," Mira told them.

"I don't know if we can keep up that long," Brightwing rasped.

"We have to try," Boreas said. "If it gets too thin we dive down."

"Why isn't Nightshade panting?" Dustbeak asked.

Mira looked at Nightshade and patted her neck. "She's a dragon. They don't really mind the thin air," she explained. "Unless it gets to where there's no oxygen at all, she'll be fine."

A few minutes later they continued their accent. Boreas could see the top, now, but he could barely breathe. The spire ended only a few wingbeats away in a sharp spike and then a flat platform. But it was almost impossible to get any higher and took a full minute to travel what they usually could in a few seconds.

As their heads poked over the top of the platform, Boreas saw what looked like a huge tree sitting atop the mountain.

He wanted to yell to the others that Mira was right. The tree was here! They found it!

But he could barely find enough strength to move his wings. The air was even thinner and each breath he gulped in only supplied him with a minuscule amount of oxygen.

"Now would be a... great time... for you to... figure out your... powers, Boreas," Mira stated between heavy breaths..

He didn't know exactly what she meant, but he didn't have time to process it. He was just a few feet away from the platform now and could almost reach out his talon and grab onto it. But his vision was going black and he couldn't feel a single muscle in his body. His head felt like it was filled with grass and he couldn't think.

He flapped his grey wings heavily and glanced at Mira. Nightshade's eyes were far away and wide, and she was panting as well. There was hardly any oxygen left in the air.

With one final gasp for air, Boreas couldn't hold on any longer and started plummeting towards the ground. He saw Brightwing lose his balance and fall sideways, smashing into Boreas and shoving him toward the mountain. Boreas felt his head slam into something very hard, and he blacked out.

CHAPTER FIVE

Boreas's eyes flickered open. There was a pale orange light filtering through the leaves above him, and it was moving slightly. As he regained consciousness, he realized he was lying on a wooden bed in a small hut. He lifted his head and looked around.

Then he remembered what had happened. A flash of memory made him lie back on the bed. *What happened after he fell? Where was he? Was Dustbeak okay?*

Boreas noticed his surroundings. The walls around him were made from wood and had patches of leaves to let in some light, and everything was tied together with vines. The roof was a thick layer of leaves in a half dome. Inside the hut was dimly lit by light outside. Boreas could see a table in the middle of the space and three chairs around it. The bed he was laying on was a large flat plank of wood covered in a thin fur, and there was a similar blanket on top of him. Nothing was this advanced in the Golden Forest, so Boreas had no clue what he was looking at.

Boreas found himself briefly wondering if Mira was all right. *Am I really worried about an elf, of all things?*

Boreas took a deep breath and lifted his head again. The door to the hut swung open and an elf with long silver hair walked in. She was carrying a lantern that filled the room with light and looked at Boreas. There were wrinkles around her eyes as she smiled at him.

Boreas sat up quickly and scooted against the wall, away from the elf. *They captured us! We must be in the elf village! Where is Dustbeak? Mira set us up!*

The elf slowly walked closer to him and set the lantern down on the table.

"You're awake," she said. Her voice was rough with age, but was still gentle. "That's good. We were worried about you."

"Where are the others?" Boreas asked the elf. He had a bad feeling that something had happened to Dustbeak.

The elf smiled again and pulled a chair close to him, sitting in it. She didn't seem afraid at all, and she also didn't seem like she wanted to hurt him.

"They're fine. My name is Anali. Don't be afraid, I won't hurt you. Mira told us what happened, and about her travels. She said how afraid griffins are of us, as though the roles were reversed and we were more capable of hurting you than you are of us," she said.

Boreas flicked his tail and stared at her, searching for any sign that she had harmful intentions. He saw none, but he kept his guard up.

"I can see you're worried," Anali said, dipping her head. "I understand. But there is no need." She paused for a moment before asking, "How do you feel? It was quite a fall. Nobody can believe all of you made it to the top of the spire in one piece."

Boreas hesitated before answering. "I'm... fine."

Anali lifted herself from the chair and held out her hand toward him. He watched her carefully, still suspicious. The elf saw the fear in his eyes and pulled back, watching him for a moment before turning back to the door.

"If you're feeling up to it, come with me. Your friends are worried about you," Anali said.

She opened the door and looked back at him before walking through, out of sight.

Boreas laid there for a few minutes, checking himself over and finding a white cloth wrapped around his back leg. He tried tugging on the cloth and found it loose; a part of it fell away and he saw a cut under it. His wings were so stiff they felt like rocks, and he had a small headache. He slid off the bed and stood, unsteady and still a bit dizzy. But he managed to walk over to the door and duck through it.

Boreas walked into a glowing dream. The hut he walked out of was only one of at least forty, all along a neat path of dirt that led in a circle. On the edge of the path were several tall wooden poles with glass boxes hanging from them, a candle in each one. Boreas saw a couple huts tucked away in the branches of trees, either ladders or staircases leading up to them from the path.

In the center of the circle was a large bonfire surrounded by elves. Boreas saw Anali walking towards them. She glanced back and grinned at him, then continued walking. He noticed Nightshade lying behind all the elves by the bonfire, watching them dance and talk and eat. He also saw two large shapes sitting just outside the firelight, watching the events with curiosity and wariness.

Boreas rushed over to them, scanning the figures for Dustbeak. There he was, sitting next to Brightwing and talking quietly. Boreas sighed with relief that his son was all right. Dustbeak looked shaken, but unharmed. Brightwing had no injuries but his feathers were ruffled and he quite looked as if he had just fallen off a mountain, which was understandable.

Dustbeak saw Boreas coming toward them and stood up, walking over to greet him.

"Dad!" he exclaimed, resting his head on Boreas's shoulder. "They said you were hurt! Are you all right?"

Boreas put a wing over his son and said, "I'm fine. But what happened?"

"After you passed out, Brightwing did too. I was starting to black out when I heard Mira yell something, and I dove down after you. Once I was low enough to breathe again, I looked up and saw that Nightshade had caught both of you. I think she accidentally cut you when she grabbed you, though," Dustbeak explained.

He flicked his tail at Boreas's leg, where the cloth was wrapped tightly around the cut. "They said that you must have hit your head or something, because you weren't waking up."

"Where's Mira?" Boreas asked.

Brightwing grunted and pointed his beak towards the fire. Boreas squinted and saw their elf friend sitting in a circle with a couple other elves, talking and laughing with them.

"The tree—I saw it," Dustbeak remembered. "It was up there! If we can find a way to keep our bearings until we get to the top, maybe we can get to the spirits."

"It would take too long," Boreas said. "I saw the tree too, but..."

"I don't think we can go back up there," Brightwing finished for him. "We have to find another way."

"There's not a tree on top of the spire!"

Boreas turned around and saw another elf, only a wingspan away. He had his arms crossed and he was frowning. His skin was dark grey and he looked about as old as Anali, but with black hair.

"Is that really what you were looking for?" the elf asked. He took a step closer to the griffins, apparently unafraid.

"Yeah..." Brightwing said slowly. "And who are you?"

"Apologies. My name is Elek. I overheard you talking about a tree... is that really why you climbed the Skyspire?" the elf implored.

"How do you know there isn't a tree up there? We saw it with our own eyes," Dustbeak argued.

"What you saw was only a trick. We know—you don't think our kind has looked for the Great Oak before? One of our more skillful warriors went to the top and returned with the news that atop the spire is nothing but a spiral of stone, arching in a way that would look like a tree if he didn't get close. It was a few years after Mira left to search for the spirits. That's why she didn't know," Elek explained calmly.

"How did you stay up there long enough to get close?" Brightwing wondered.

Elek smiled. "He was a rider, like Mira. Dragons can last much longer in high altitudes than the rest of us."

"But, how did he find out? Even riding, Mira was close to passing out. I don't think even she could last long enough to get close to the tree," Boreas pointed out.

Elek looked at him and narrowed his eyes. He looked confused, like there was something they should have known already. After a few seconds of hesitation, he said, "I think that information is better shared by Mira. If she hasn't already told you, there must be a reason. I suggest asking her."

Dustbeak's tail slowly curved around his leg, like it sometimes did when he was thinking hard and not paying attention to anything else. Boreas liked that about him—it was one of the few things that had stuck with him since he was a hatchling.

Once Elek walked away, Boreas turned back to the others. "So where do we go next?"

"Definitely *not* the Charponds," Brightwing said, flicking his wings. "I'm not going through the Fangrocks on a slight chance it might be there."

"Remember what Mira said when we met her? About our connection to the spirits?" Dustbeak asked.

"She could control the fire," Boreas remembered.

"And the whole reason she dragged me along is because of my connection to the sun spirit," Brightwing said, a bit begrudgingly. "She said that together, maybe the two of us could find them."

"How long would that take?" asked Dustbeak. "To control your connection? If you could learn, we wouldn't need to search all these places. Maybe you could just talk to the spirits and know where they are."

Brightwing shook his head. "I've never had any signs of being able to do that kind of thing. I hardly even feel the spirit."

"We have to try," Boreas said.

He was surprised at himself for being this engaged in the journey. Only three days ago he was terrified of Mira and her dragon, and now he was willingly going along with them, like they were old friends and he had nothing to fear. He was still afraid of Nightshade, and he knew Mira was holding back information. But for some reason, he trusted that they were doing the right thing. And somehow he felt that Mira really did have the intention of saving the spirits, and that's all she wanted to do.

Later that night, the griffins slept outside next to the doused fire. They were offered places inside the huts from some of the braver elves, but turned them down. They didn't get a chance to talk to Mira other than her walking over to them to say they would be leaving in the morning.

Boreas woke up to voices. He raised his head and looked around, seeing two elves outside one of the huts talking. He couldn't hear what they were saying, but finally they walked inside and didn't notice him.

Soon Mira appeared out of one of the huts, with Keko behind her. They walked over to the griffins and Keko stayed behind her sister, peeking out at them.

"Keko, they're not going to hurt you," Mira laughed.

Keko looked up at her and whined, "I know that! I'm just... watching from a distance, is all."

Mira chuckled and shook her head, then put her hands on her hips and looked at Boreas. "So, what did you three decide?"

"You mean after we almost fell off a cliff and woke up in an elf village?" Boreas asked.

Mira let one of her arms down and raised an eyebrow. "I think you mean, 'thank you Mira for saving our lives and catching us. Wow, you really *aren't* an evil elf plotting to kill us all.'"

Boreas opened his mouth to argue, but she continued. "Yes, I know that's what you all think of me. But no matter how you put it, I'm *not going to hurt you*, Boreas. Unless you get on my nerves, then you'll feel some pain."

"To be fair, you did leave us alone in an unfamiliar forest full of elves," Dustbeak said unexpectedly. He had woken up part way through the conversation.

"What, I can't catch up with my family?" Mira argued. "Wouldn't you want to talk to Silverpelt if you hadn't seen her in eleven years?"

Boreas's heart skipped a beat. "Eleven years?" he whispered.

Mira nodded, her anger fading. "Once Nightshade was big enough, we left home to search for the spirits. We rarely visit; the last time we were here was six years ago."

"I'm sorry," Boreas said. "We've been treating you unfairly."

Mira shook her head and looked away. "Let's get started."

"Last night we thought that it would be best to go to Quake Canyon," Dustbeak said after a moment.

Brightwing stirred, then sat up a few seconds later as Mira said, "All right, but we'll have to cross the Scorchwood Valley." She opened her sack and pulled out the map again. "Or, I guess now that we're close to the Skyspire we could go around the Skyspire Mountains and Edgewater Shore. The tree is said to be on the Northern end, though, so if we do go that way we have to fly through the length of the canyon."

"So either through the desert, or the long way through the canyon," Brightwing observed.

Mira thought for a moment. Then she spoke. "Whichever way we choose, I think it's time I start training you."

"Training?" Boreas echoed.

Mira nodded. "To use the spirits." She turned to Boreas. "For you it will be the sky. Once mastered, you could do anything from making a breeze to creating oxygen."

Boreas took a moment to think about that. Was it really possible?

Looking at Dustbeak, she continued. "And for you it's the land. You might be able to do something as strong as cause an earthquake." When Dustbeak's jaw dropped practically to the floor, she added, "After almost a century of practice, of course."

"What can you do?" Brightwing asked.

"So far, the most I can do is hold a flame and control what it does. No one knows the limits of the spirits, or if they even have any. Who knows, with the sun spirit, maybe one day you could drive away the rain and bring a clear sky. I don't even know the extent of my own powers. But for now, we have to get to Quake Canyon."

Boreas thought for a moment. If they went across the desert, it would be faster but they would have to fight for food and water, and avoid sandents. But if they went around, the journey would be much safer, though longer as well. Then again, a longer, safer journey could give them more time to train.

"I think we should go the long way around," he said at last, then explained his reasons.

Mira nodded and crossed her arms. "And on our way, hopefully you three can learn something about the spirits."

~~~

They left the elf village after Mira got a fresh supply of food and resources in her bag. It took a few hours to exit the forest, but now they were at the treeline. All Boreas could see to their right was a seemingly endless ocean of sand. In front of them was the Skyspire Mountains, which they would pass through before going around the Sandeep Plateau.

"The mountains are treacherous normally, but I know the way through them, so it should be a breeze," Mira was saying.

"What's so dangerous about them?" Dustbeak asked anxiously.

"Well, for starters, there are quicksand pots all throughout them. The rocks can be incredibly sharp in places, and from the ground it might as well be a maze with no exit. But we're going to stay as close to the Skyspire as possible, where there are plenty of cliffs to stay above all that," Mira explained.

The elf climbed atop Nightshade and they flew toward the mountains. Boreas tried to focus on the wind in his feathers and the air under his wings, but he didn't feel any kind of spiritual energy like Mira said he might.

They flew in silence for an hour. Boreas guessed everyone else was trying to focus on the spirits as well, but it didn't look like the other griffins were having much luck.

Finally Mira broke the spell by calling, "We'll go on foot for a while."
~~~

Boreas was glad to hear this. His wings were aching from the long flight yesterday, and they felt like they were going to fall off.

They landed on a thin ledge and started walking along it. Boreas made sure to watch where he was putting each foot, nervous about falling and not being able to regain his balance. The rock was barely thick enough for Nightshade's talons.

They went on walking until the sun had reached its peak in the sky. The mountains behind them had been blocking the sun when it was low, but now the heat pounded down on them relentlessly. Boreas looked ahead of them but saw no indication that they were nearing the end of the mountain range.

"Now would be the perfect time to gain a little control over your hidden abilities," Mira said suddenly. "All the elements are here. Dustbeak, try to focus on the rocks beneath your feet, the mountains around you. Boreas, think about the sky and the air going in and out of your lungs. And Brightwing—"

"The sun is already making me miserable enough, I don't want to focus on it more," Brightwing complained.

"Do you want to communicate with the spirits or not?" Mira asked.

Brightwing muttered something under his breath and Mira continued, "As I was saying, focus on the sun. Try to feel every bit of warmth it's giving you, and see if you can feel anything from it."

Boreas had been trying the entire time to get in touch with the sky, but nothing seemed to be working. They fell into silence once again, this time for almost two hours. Replacing the steep drop into the mountain, here there was a long crevasse lined with sharp rocks, making the thought of falling even more frightening.

Then Boreas heard Brightwing yelp. He turned and saw that the ground had cracked underneath him, putting him off-balance. The black griffin started tipping towards the steep drop to his left.

Dustbeak was closest and reached out to grab Brightwing's talon, but he had already started to fall over the edge and he only pulled Dustbeak down with him.

"Dustbeak! Brightwing!" Boreas yelled, making Mira turn in surprise.

Brightwing was dangling over the edge now, and the only thing keeping him from falling into the spiky crevasse was Dustbeak. But Boreas's son was starting to slip over the rocks.

"Hold on, Dustbeak!" Boreas yelled.

He rushed over to his son and grabbed his back leg to keep him up.

Brightwing was scrambling to grab hold of something with his back feet, but it was a sheer drop into the crevasse. There were sharp rocks lining the wall behind him preventing him from spreading his wings.

"Mira, do something!" Boreas shouted.

"Dad, I'm slipping!" Dustbeak yelled.

Boreas saw long claw marks in the stone beneath his son's feet. He glanced back at his dad with a terrified expression.

"Just hold on, Dustbeak," Boreas said.

He didn't remember a time before this when he had ever seen terror in Dustbeak's eyes. If they couldn't haul him up, he would drop onto the deadly rocks below.

"Mira, HURRY!" Brightwing yelled, his back feet flailing for a foothold.

Boreas glanced at Mira and saw her quickly tying together thick vines to use as a rope. It was almost long enough to reach Brightwing. Nightshade was pacing nervously around them, her talons just barely too wide to reach down and grab Brightwing.

Then Dustbeak's leg slipped out of Boreas's talons, and he and Brightwing fell into the crevasse.

Boreas yelled after him. "NO!"

CHAPTER SIX

Everything after that moment was a blur.

Boreas didn't know what he did. Only that he felt a surge of energy force its way through him, and a gust of wind almost knocked him off his feet.

Then Dustbeak and Brightwing stopped falling for a split second, just a moment away from hitting the jagged rocks. Everything seemed to go in slow motion for Boreas, and he didn't know what was happening.

The rocks around them cracked, the sharp tips falling into the hole. Then Boreas could breathe again, and Dustbeak spread his wings and soared out of the crevasse, followed by Brightwing.

He landed next to Boreas and laid on the ground, breathing heavily and digging his claws into the stone. Brightwing latched his claws into the furthest place he could find from the edge. All Boreas could do was stand there.

What just happened?

They sat there until Dustbeak got his bearings, then decided it was safer to fly the rest of the way until they reached Edgewater Shore, even though their wings were all sore from the previous days.

As they flew, all Boreas could think about was what had happened. The sky was dead silent. He guessed everyone else was pondering this as well.

Finally the mountains ebbed away to gravel, then sand. They landed on the beach to rest. Boreas had only stood on sand a few times. This was different from the sand in the Scorchwood Valley or the riverbed. It was much softer and slightly wet.

"Can we stop ignoring what just happened?" Brightwing said anxiously.

"Yeah, what *was* that?" Dustbeak agreed.

Everyone looked at Boreas. There was a small trace of a smile on Mira's face, he thought.

"I... don't know," Boreas admitted.

"I do," Mira said, dismounting Nightshade. "*That*, Boreas, was the sky spirit."

"You mean... *I* did that?" Boreas asked.

He knew it was true. He had felt something back there, but it was still hard to believe.

Mira nodded. "Sometimes you can't even think about what you're doing. It just sort of happens, especially when something you care about is in danger. You saved Dustbeak and Brightwing."

Boreas stood still. He didn't know what to think, especially with everyone staring at him like this.

Finally Brightwing spoke up, clearly trying to change the subject. "I think we should stay here for the night. We can get an early start tomorrow."

He gave Boreas a strange look before turning around and walking toward the ocean.

"I'll get some firewood," Dustbeak offered.

He walked off toward the base of the mountain, where a few trees were growing out of the cracks.

Boreas turned back to Mira. "Why are they acting like this?"

He felt like the other griffins had some sort of grudge against him.

"It can be hard watching someone else achieve something before yourself. They just want to be able to understand," Mira said. She smiled at him. "Trust me, I know. But they'll get it."

Boreas looked at Dustbeak, who was picking up loose sticks from the ground.

"I hope so," he said.

That night they ate fish from the ocean and quietly stared into the fire. Boreas stayed awake long after everyone else was asleep. He couldn't shake the feeling that Dustbeak and Brightwing had something against him now, even though he didn't even know what he did. He had thought that he and Dustbeak were getting closer since they left the Golden Forest, but it all might have been undone now.

Finally, late in the night, he fell asleep listening to the waves crash against the shore, then roll back into the sea. He slept uneasily, dreaming about things that he couldn't remember when he woke up. At last the sun appeared over the eastern horizon, and the others started to wake up. Boreas had been awake for almost an hour now, not being able to fall back asleep after his last nightmare.

"Morning," Dustbeak said to them.

Boreas nodded to them and Brightwing mumbled something, stretching out his wings.

"All right, we have a long flight ahead of us," Mira said, checking over her bag. "We should probably catch more fish. It'll be at least three days until we get to the other side of the canyon, and as far as I know there's not really any water source there unless we fly over the Redrocks to the ocean. That means not much food and hardly any water."

"We can stand drinking saltwater for a little while, but what about you?" Boreas asked. Griffins had a natural ability to be able to survive off saltwater for a while, but Boreas didn't think elves could.

"I have a few canteens of water that I refilled in the village," Mira said. "If I conserve it, they should last me more than a week. I'll be fine."

"I can go fishing," Brightwing offered.

"I'll help," Dustbeak said.

They walked towards the water. Boreas watched them go and sighed. When would they forgive him, and what did they even need to forgive him for? He didn't understand why saving the two of them—completely by accident—could cause so much conflict.

"They'll come around," Mira reassured him. "But this is no time to stop working on your powers. All three of you need to keep practicing. Hopefully by the time we reach the northern end of the canyon, you'll all be able to control it. And if Brightwing would just let the spirit flow, we might be able to locate the tree without having to search all of Arcenti for it."

"What do you mean?" Boreas wondered.

"You can't tell?" Mira asked. "He's completely blocking the spirit. I think he might be scared of something, or just refusing to do it. But he's definitely not letting his powers come. All that anger he's showing to you is just frustration at himself. I have no clue why he would be doing that, though."

Mira walked away to situate Nightshade's saddle. Boreas watched Brightwing claw at a fish under the surface of the water. Why could this old griffin, who seemed to want nothing but to save the spirits and go home, want to block his abilities?

When the two griffins returned from fishing, their fur wet and smelling of salt, they started their flight. Within an hour they could see the dark brown rocks of the canyon ahead of them, and by midday they were just a few miles away from it. They stopped to rest, then continued their flight. Once they were over the canyon, Boreas decided to continue to focus on the wind under his wings, even though it could increase the conflict between him and the other griffins. He felt it would be better to learn faster than stop now and wait. What if he needed to use it again, and didn't know how?

He flew just below and in front of Dustbeak, listening to his breathing and wondering what his son was thinking about. They landed on the edge of the canyon and walked until the sun was high in the sky, then continued flying. They flew until the sun was sinking to their left. Boreas's wings had been through so much flying in the past days that they felt numb as he landed.

The next two days dragged on. They alternated flying and walking depending on how hot it was, walking in the cooler hours of the day and getting wind when the sun was high. By the time they reached the Northern end, Dustbeak had told them that he felt *something*, but he couldn't figure out how to bring it out.

Now they were settling themselves on the warm rocks and watching the moon rise. Boreas thought of Silverpelt again, missing her kind eyes and her beautiful voice.

Mira hadn't made a fire because it had been a hot day and they were all looking forward to a cool night. They ate two of the fish Mira had packed. They were all thirsty and had a few sips of Mira's water, but they didn't want to waste it.

In the morning they flew the last few hours to the end of the canyon. As they landed on the edge, Boreas felt hopeless. There wasn't a plant in sight.

"It's not here!" Brightwing bellowed. "We came all this way for nothing!"

Dustbeak fluffed up his wings and dug his talons into the ground. "It wasn't at the Skyspire, and it's not at Quake Canyon. What makes us think it will be anywhere we go? We've gone halfway across Arcenti, and we're nowhere closer to finding the spirits! How do we even know the spirits are in a tree? This is all based on some great legend, right? I'm done flying around chasing a story!"

The ground below Dustbeak seemed to shake slightly, and there was a loud rumble from around them.

"Dustbeak!" Boreas yelled

"Dustbeak, pay attention!" Brightwing called, jumping back as the ground began to crack.

Mira pointed at Dustbeak and Nightshade immediately ran forward and reached toward Dustbeak to try to get his attention, as he clearly wasn't paying attention to what he was doing. But the crack in the stone was growing and it reached Nightshade's talons before she could reach him. The rock splintered apart around Dustbeak, and only when it shifted underneath him did he snap out of his rage. He looked down with shock as the slab of rock below him started to move.

"Dustbeak!" Boreas yelled again, rushing toward his son.

Mira grabbed his wing to stop him, but he flung her off. *Not again! What if I can't save him this time?*

As Boreas reached Dustbeak, Dustbeak looked up and yelled, "Dad, stop!"

It was too late. The rock underneath them gave away, and they plummeted into the empty space below.

~~~

Boreas saw only darkness. The light had disappeared so fast as they plummeted into the pit. After a moment his eyes adjusted and he saw Dustbeak lying on his side a few feet away.

Boreas staggered to his feet and ran over to Dustbeak, shaking his shoulder.

"Dustbeak!" Boreas exclaimed. "Dustbeak, are you okay?"

Dustbeak groaned and moved his head towards his body, wincing. Boreas sighed and looked around. He couldn't see anything around them except a shaft of light coming from above. He looked into it but saw nothing. A moment later he heard an echoing voice.

"Boreas! Dustbeak! Are you there?" It was Mira. Her voice sounded far away, and if it wasn't for the echo he might not have heard her.

"We're here!" Boreas yelled.

Mira's voice came several seconds later. "Can you fly back up?"

"Maybe, but Dustbeak's hurt," Boreas said.

"How far down are you?" Mira called back. "Maybe Nightshade and I can get you out, if we widen the hole a bit."

Boreas craned his neck to see anything but the faint light, but he couldn't see the top of the pit.

"It's far," he said.

Mira was quiet for a long time. Then she shouted down, "Do you think there's any other way out?"
~~~

"I can't see a thing," Boreas stated.

Dust floated into his throat and he coughed.

"I can send you down a fire," Mira said after hesitating for a while. "If I light a stick and toss it down, and you just make sure you're out of the way, it will light up the pit."

"Won't it go out?"

"Not if I can keep it going from up here. It's not a guarantee, but it's worth a try. If it works you won't have to wander around in complete darkness."

Boreas thought for a while. From what he could tell, the cavern seemed wide enough for them to stay far away from the torch when she dropped it.

"Okay," Boreas yelled to her. "Tell me when you're going to throw it."

Mira grew quiet, and Boreas waited for her to light the torch. He crouched by Dustbeak.

"Come on," he whispered. "We have to move."

Dustbeak said nothing, so Boreas nudged him. He winced and made a whimpering sound.

"We have to move," Boreas pleaded. "Can you walk?"

"Maybe," Dustbeak said slowly.

His shoulders shook as he tried hoisting himself to his feet, but he fell back against the ground with a loud thump.

"Boreas, look out!" Mira screamed.

Boreas turned and saw a small flicker of firelight falling toward them, and fast. He jumped up pushed Dustbeak across the floor, out of the light. Boreas glanced at the flame and leapt toward the shadows. He was an inch away from safety when the torch landed, spewing sparks as the wood splintered. A shower of sparks landed on his wing and tail. Boreas yelled and threw himself onto the ground, batting out the fire before it burned him.

"Sorry!" Mira yelled. "I dropped it!"

Boreas grunted and said, "We're fine."

He ran back over to his son, bringing the torch with him. The fire had gone out but the end was still glowing, so it produced a small amount of light.

"Where does it hurt?" Boreas asked, setting the torch next to his son.

Dustbeak lifted his head slightly. "Mrrf... Everywhere," he groaned.

Boreas squinted and saw Dustbeak's back leg twisted in an awkward position. When he reached for it, Dustbeak winced.

"I think your leg is broken," Boreas diagnosed. "Can you move it so it's less twisted?"

Dustbeak shifted his position slightly but gasped and fell back to the ground.

"It hurts," he whimpered.

"I know, I know," Boreas said, trying to console his son.

He knew nothing about healing. Whenever griffins got hurt in the Golden Forest, the injury usually healed by itself. If it didn't, there were a few griffins who knew how to treat wounds. But Boreas had no experience with anything like this, so he had no clue what to do.

"Mira!" Boreas yelled. "I think his leg is broken. What should I do?"

It took a while for Mira to respond.

Finally she answered, "Try to keep it straight. If there's anything to tie a stick or something to it, try that."

Boreas looked around in the dwindling light of the torch. He could only see rubble from the falling rocks.

"Do you have anything?" he asked Mira.

A moment later she yelled, "Catch!" and dropped down a small leather pouch.

Boreas caught it and looked inside, where there was a length of thick vine, different sizes of sticks, and a few leaves.

"Find the stick that's closest to the length of his leg," Mira instructed, "and put it against the broken part."

Boreas followed her instructions and found a stick that was a good size, bringing it over to Dustbeak. His son winced as he lay the stick against his leg, but didn't pull away.

"Now what?" Boreas asked.

"Now position the stick so it will keep his leg straight, but so he can still move it. Then tie it to him with the vine," Mira told him.

Boreas did what she said, carefully moving Dustbeak's leg to fit the make-shift cast.

When it was tied together, he asked, "Is that all right? Does it hurt?"

"It constantly hurts," Dustbeak pointed out. "But... that's better. Thank you."

"Boreas, is it done?" Mira asked.

"Yes," Boreas answered. "What are the leaves for?"

"Have him eat them. They'll ease the pain."

Boreas took the leaves out of the bag and handed them to Dustbeak, who took them cautiously but started chewing on them with an expression on his face that suggested they tasted terrible.

"Under the leaves there should also be a thick green plant. You can share it—it has water in it. Be careful though because it could have some thorns on it. I forgot I had it in my medicine bag until I threw it down," Mira added.

Boreas looked again. Sure enough, wrapped in a cloth was the thick green ball. He took it out gently, avoiding the sharp spines along its ridges.

"How many of these do you have?" Boreas wondered. "They could solve our water problem."

"I had two in my emergency pouch, and that's one of them. Each has enough water for three, but they might be a little dried out. I got them from the Scorchwood Valley," Mira said.

Boreas used his claw to slice the plant in half and handed it to Dustbeak, who had finished choking down the leaves. He gratefully took a sip, then handed it back to Boreas. Boreas took a small drink. The water was cool and refreshing, and he wanted to keep drinking. But he knew they should conserve all the water they had.

"How are we going to get out?" Dustbeak asked.

The leaves must have been kicking in, because he lifted his head again and shifted positions a bit to be more comfortable. "Is the hole big enough to fly through?"

"I don't think so," Boreas said. "We'll have to find another way."

Dustbeak looked around. The light that had been coming into the pit was fading now, so the sun was probably close to setting. Soon they would be in complete darkness.

"We need some light," Dustbeak said, seeing Boreas's worried look. "Should we try the torch again?"

"It went out as soon as it hit," Boreas said. "We got lucky last time that the fire didn't catch. I don't think we should risk it again."

Dustbeak nodded thoughtfully. "Maybe this isn't just a sinkhole. There could be an exit somewhere."

Boreas had an idea. "When we fell down, *you* were cracking the rocks. You used your power," he said.

Dustbeak shrank back and his head drooped. "I—I didn't know... Why are you bringing this up?"

"No, that's not my point. My point is that if you can do that again, you could make us a way out of here," Boreas said quickly.

Dustbeak brightened a little, but then the grim look on his face came back. "But, I don't know how I did it. I just looked down, and the rocks were cracking..."

"It's all right," Boreas said, putting a wing over his son's shoulder. "It wasn't your fault. But if you can summon it again, it could be our way out."

Dustbeak sighed and closed his eyes. They sat in silence for a few moments, then Dustbeak struggled to his feet.

"We have to try," he said.

Boreas stood and followed Dustbeak to the middle of the sinkhole. Dustbeak walked slowly and stopped for a heartbeat every few steps, so Boreas assumed his leg was still giving him pain.

When they were standing below the hole, Dustbeak closed his eyes and tensed, his claws scratching the rock below him.

After several seconds, Dustbeak let out his breath and his shoulders dropped. "Nothing's happening," he said disappointedly. "I can feel it—it's definitely there, but I can't fish it out."

"Hey, it's not your fault," Boreas repeated. "You'll figure it out, we all will. But until then we need to make a new plan."

Mira's observation came back to Boreas's mind. Was Brightwing really blocking his abilities? He pushed the thought away. Boreas couldn't worry about that now, though he wondered what Brightwing was doing now that he and Dustbeak were trapped. Why wasn't he trying to help?

"I'll look around," Boreas said. He made his way toward the shadowed area, feeling his path when it got too dark.

After a while, his talon slipped down an edge in the floor. He felt around it and found a cliff-like drop, but it was only about a foot tall. He stepped onto the ledge beneath it and found another drop. A staircase?

"I found something," Boreas called.

"I did too," Dustbeak answered.

Boreas returned to Dustbeak. There was still a bit of light coming from the hole, and Boreas could see stars far, far above. The full moon was producing plenty of light above, but down in the pit barely any of it hit the ground. It was enough to see where they were stepping in a small circle, but everything else was dark.

Boreas found where Dustbeak was feeling and put his talon on the wall beside Dustbeak's.

"It's some kind of carving," Dustbeak said, running his talon across the stone.

Boreas followed his movements and felt clean cuts in the rock. He couldn't tell what the carving was, but there was definitely something etched on the wall. That added to the stairs... had someone been here before?

"What did you find?" Dustbeak asked.

Boreas led him to the stairs, and they descended them cautiously.

"This is so strange," Dustbeak said, keeping a wing over Boreas for support. "There's no way it's natural. Elves, maybe?"

Boreas said nothing. He was deep in thought. What could have made these? It could have been elves, as they were the most advanced species on Arcenti. But it was still weird. Why would they make a carving and a staircase in a seemingly unreachable pit?

When they reached the bottom of the stairs, the space was lit up slightly. Boreas couldn't tell where the light was coming from. It was constant, not flickering, so it couldn't be a fire.

They couldn't see anything else strange about the cavern. From what the light illuminated, it was just a big empty cave. But then something caught Boreas's eye.

A shadow was moving slowly across the edge of the lighted area.

"Careful," he hissed under his breath.

Boreas flicked his tail toward the shadow and Dustbeak stepped back nervously.

The shadow slithered towards them silently, and Boreas spotted a figure poised just out of sight.

They weren't alone in the cave.

CHAPTER SEVEN

The shadow was getting closer by the second. Boreas couldn't see what was making it, but it was slowly moving toward them.

The two griffins watched the shadow inch closer. Boreas put his wing in front of Dustbeak in case he needed to protect him.

Then someone stepped out of the darkness.

It was a large griffin with jet black fur and dark grey feathers. His eyes were narrowed and he was growling. Boreas noticed something strange about the griffin's eyes. They were pitch black, like a shadow had consumed them.

"Thank goodness," Boreas said in a friendly tone. "It's another griffin."

Dustbeak glanced at Boreas with uncertainty. Boreas knew what he was feeling. Despite his positive greeting, he knew something was wrong. This griffin didn't look friendly. But he continued, holding on to the hope that maybe he was just frightened by Boreas and Dustbeak, and that's why he was angry.

"Do you know a way out of here?" Boreas asked, trying to sound non-threatening.

The dark griffin stared at them for several seconds, his eyes showing nothing but aggression. Boreas prepared to run.

Finally the stranger spoke. "You have come for the spirits."

A chill went down Boreas's spine. The griffin's voice was deep and scratchy, and it sounded like it alone could kill someone, never mind the terrifying body it came from.

"N—no," Dustbeak stammered. "We just want to get out of here."

The griffin bent down and narrowed his eyes further, his tail lashing.

"Dustbeak," Boreas whispered, "*Run*."

"I—"

"Just *run*!"

Dustbeak pivoted and sprinted back up the stairs, but stumbled every few steps. His leg was wobbly and was still hurting him, by the sound of it. Boreas wanted to help him, but the strange griffin was running toward him with his claws out.

Boreas ducked and rolled to avoid the sharp talons. He turned around and saw Dustbeak scrambling out of the way and the griffin just a few steps behind him.

Boreas leapt on top of the griffin and bit his shoulder but immediately got flung off. He landed on his side and rushed to his feet, narrowly avoiding another attack.

"Who are you?" Boreas cried as he took a blow to the side.

The griffin said nothing, only tackled Boreas and sunk his claws into his leg. Boreas pulled away quickly, his leg stinging. The griffin had hit directly where Nightshade had cut Boreas after his fall.

"I don't want to fight!" Boreas yelled at his attacker.

Still, the mysterious griffin said nothing and continued attacking. He hit Boreas's wound again. Boreas knew that he was targeting his leg. Somehow this griffin sensed Boreas's weakness.

Boreas swiped at the griffin again, leaving a cut above his eye. He seemed to not even feel the wound and didn't flinch. Boreas pelted him with attacks and finally knocked him to the floor. Taking the opportunity to look behind him, Boreas saw that Dustbeak had made it to the top of the stairs and disappeared into the dark tunnel.

He felt claws in his back and whipped back around, biting the griffin's ear. It bit him back, leaving a mark on Boreas's neck. He felt a warm trickle of blood run down to his shoulder.

Boreas tried to hold the griffin back as long as he could, but he couldn't fight someone who didn't seem to feel pain and knew every weakness.

The griffin tackled Boreas and flipped him onto his back. Boreas didn't know how much fight he had left. The dark griffin reeled his head back and prepared for one final bite to the neck. Boreas squirmed under his huge talons but he couldn't get free. He was too injured and tired to think.

There was a blinding flash of light, and Boreas had to close his eyes. A wave of heat went over him and the griffin he was fighting.

Boreas heard a thundering roar and the pressure on his stomach was lifted as the griffin jumped off of him. He staggered to his feet and squinted into the light, which was coming from the top of the staircase. His opponent was stalking toward the light, growling.

Then Mira and Nightshade raced down the stairs, Mira holding a ball of fire in front of her. The griffin was unfazed and immediately hurdled over the bottom few steps to attack Mira, but she only raised the fire in front of her and left the griffin flying backwards, the fur on his stomach smoking.

Boreas watched as Nightshade tackled the griffin out of the air. Only a few moments later, he was lying on the ground, dead.

"What—" Boreas began.

"A shade," Mira said quietly.

"A what?" Boreas asked. He saw Dustbeak beginning to limp down the stairs and rushed to help him.

"Someone who has been completely taken over by the dark spirit," Mira explained. "Once that happens, there's only one way to stop them."

"How did you and Nightshade get in?" Boreas asked, sitting next to Dustbeak.

"Dustbeak collapsed the ceiling. He said there wasn't enough time to find another entrance," Mira said.

Her voice sounded far away and she was looking at the ground, thinking hard.

Boreas looked at his son, who smiled shyly. He nodded at Dustbeak and smiled back. There was a cough from the top of the stairs, and Boreas sprang up to fight whoever it was. But it was just Brightwing.

"So much dust," Brightwing complained, coughing a few more times. "I found another tunnel, but I guess you don't need it anymore."

"The shade—it said something before it attacked us," Dustbeak said. "Something about the spirits."

"It asked if we came for them," Boreas remembered. "Why? Could he have meant that the tree really is here?"

Mira didn't seem to register what they had said.

"Mira?" Brightwing asked.

The elf looked up and muttered, "Sorry, what?"

"The shade," Dustbeak repeated. "It asked if we were here for the spirits. Does that mean the tree is here?"

Mira thought for a moment, then shook her head. "I don't feel anything. And I don't see how a tree could grow down here."

"What if they aren't in a tree?" Brightwing suggested. "They could just be down here, hiding."

Boreas remembered the carving that Dustbeak had found. If the shade had been here because of the spirits, maybe the carving had something to do with them. He got up and led the others into the first room. The wall with the carving luckily hadn't been destroyed, but there was debris everywhere. It took them a while to move the biggest rocks out of the way to see the engraving.

Carved in the wall was what looked like a story line. There was a cliff face, with what must have been the spirits standing on top, each of them a different, almost animal-looking figure.

They were looking at the sky, where there was another spirit floating above them. This one had sharp, zig-zagging lines extending from it. The next piece of the story was the spirits running away from the cliff, and the sun rising in the back. Where the other spirit had been there were now dots scattered around.

There was a spot on the wall that looked like an empty desert, and after it were the spirits again. They were gathered around a huge tree, probably the Great Oak. In the middle of the spirits was a griffin. Then, in the next panel, the spirits were gone, and the griffin stood alone in the forest with small star shapes around it.

"What..." Brightwing trailed off.

"It's the Golden Forest!" Mira exclaimed. "The Great Oak is in the Golden Forest!"

"I think we would know if the spirits lived with us," Dustbeak said. "You said it yourself."

"Not if they're being hidden." Mira pointed at the griffin in the picture. "A guard. That's what we haven't thought about yet. The spirits chose someone to guard them, to keep them a secret."

"How can you tell it's the Golden Forest?" Boreas asked.

Mira gestured to the trees around the griffin in the last picture. "The Silver Forest is more dense. And the Glistening Forest and Shadowsnow woods look nothing like this. You can see the river in the back, too. And it's right next to the Scorchwood Valley, and there's a griffin."

"It's just a picture. We don't know that this is what the place really looks like," Brightwing said.

"But if the cliff face in the carving is Quake Canyon, then there's a high chance that the spirits were here. They made this map and this cave," Mira said. "And if the spirits made it, then it has to be accurate!"

"Or it's another trick," Boreas said. He wanted to believe this just as much as Mira did, but was it really this easy? Was it there all along?

"I don't think so," Mira argued. "Boreas, I know you don't fully trust me. But I really believe that it's there."

"Besides, where would we have gone next anyway? The Charponds? It's on the way," Dustbeak said, his eyes having a new spark in them.

Boreas nodded. "I guess it couldn't hurt," he said.

He thought about what Mira had said. Did he trust her fully? He remembered when she had first cornered him and Dustbeak, how scared he had been for him and his son's life. But now he found it easy to believe what she said and go along with her. Why? Because he had been with her long enough to see the good in her? Because she had saved him?

Or maybe, even though he hadn't realized it, they had become friends.

Once they had made their decision, Mira mounted Nightshade and they flew out of the now much-bigger hole. Boreas hung back for a moment, tracing his claw along the stone.

He would have loved to see this.

Once he had made a noticeable scratch, Boreas followed his friends.

He reached the top of the sinkhole and was impressed with Dustbeak for clearing out this much rock on his own, and it was only his second time using his powers—and the first time using them on purpose. He caught up to his friends and Brightwing rolled his wings, muttering something to himself.

They started their journey once again, deciding this time to cut across the Scorchwood Valley. They designed their flight on Mira's map, planning to hop from one oasis to another until they reached the Golden Forest. They were far apart, but Mira guessed they could reach each one in less than two days.

With the sun rising ahead of them, they started flying toward the desert. They had crossed the Sandeep Plateau by the time the sun was climbing the sky, and before he knew it Boreas could already see the first oasis.

At midday they landed at the oasis and drank all the water they could. They rested their wings until the sun was behind them, then set off again. By nightfall Boreas had grown exhausted of the heat and welcomed the coolness and darkness of the night. His wings were past numb now and felt nothing.

The next day was rough for all of them. The coolness the night brought was replaced with immense heat and exhaustion. They wouldn't be able to reach the next oasis till sunset, according to Mira. Boreas tried to focus on anything but the heat as they flew, but it was impossible.

"Hey, any chance you're doing this?" he asked Brightwing, who was flying above him. "If you are, could you stop?"

Brightwing glared down at him and said nothing. Boreas frowned. This old griffin couldn't take a joke.

Again Mira's words returned to Boreas. He decided to think about that instead of the long flight, although it wasn't much better. After two full hours of contemplating why Brightwing would be avoiding his powers, Boreas had gotten nowhere. The best he could think of was that Brightwing was scared, but that didn't seem very likely.

At last they were at the oasis, and the sun was getting low. Boreas dove toward the water without waiting for the others and landed in the shallow pond, bending his head down to drink. Everyone else joined him and they enjoyed the shade that the Scorchwood trees provided.

"When the moon is up, we'll leave again," Mira said after they finished drinking. "I'd like to stay a little longer, but it's best if we make the most of the night."

"Couldn't we walk for a while?" Dustbeak asked, his wings hanging like bags of rocks from his shoulders.

"It's too risky. Sandents could sneak up on us with ease, especially during the day when the sand is hot and the heat is messing up our minds," Mira said.

Boreas thought of the sand-dwelling creatures. He had never seen one, and he was lucky for that. They had quite the reputation for being one of the most deadly things in the Scorchwood Valley. The long snake-like predators lived underground and burrowed through the sand to hunt. Once they caught whatever they were hunting, their jaws would clamp down and nothing could escape. Although their small eyes were nearly useless, their sense of smell could trace prey from miles away, and they could feel the vibrations of anything moving on the sand above them. Some stories said that they could detect a grain of sand moving in the wind.

Dustbeak was clearly thinking of this too, because he shuddered and rolled his shoulders, limping to the water for another drink.

Boreas curled up on the sand to rest until they were ready to leave again, and Mira gave Dustbeak the last of the herbs for the pain in his leg. Dustbeak woke him up when the moon was climbing the sky and they started flying again. If they flew hard and fast, they could reach the last oasis by sunset the next day. Boreas looked at the moon and sighed. I'm coming, Silverpelt. We're almost home.

This time they had a bit of conversation during their flight. Dustbeak brought up the topic of what they were going to do when they actually found the spirits. Mira suggested that they try to communicate with them and convince them to fight the darkness, like they did all those years ago. Through all this, Brightwing remained silent. He seemed distant and distracted, like he was listening to tiny whispers in his ears.

Finally, the Golden Forest was in sight. Boreas could see the treeline where he had once stood, watching the rest of the world from the safety of his home. Never had he imagined seeing it like this, alongside an elf and a dragon, flying back towards it.

That reminded him about something Elek had said the night they were in the elf village. He had been guarding something about Mira and Nightshade.

But that thought left Boreas's mind as they neared the forest. Mira told them to land at the oasis first, to regroup and make a plan. Boreas sighed and slowly made his way to the ground, landing on the hot sand carefully and rushing to the shade of the Scorchwood trees. The sun was beginning to set, but the sand was still scorching hot.

"So, according to the carving, the tree should be in a thin part of the forest, by a river," Mira said.

"How will we know which one it is?" Brightwing asked.

"What about the guard?" Dustbeak suggested. "If we depicted the story correctly, there should be someone guarding the spirits. A griffin, most likely."

“Do you know anyone that could possibly be hiding them?” Mira asked.

Dustbeak thought for a moment.

“No,” he said slowly. “But Ashfeather knows more about the spirits than anyone in the Golden Forest, at least that I’ve talked to. Maybe she could help us.”

Boreas nodded. As much as he hadn’t trusted Ashfeather, Dustbeak was right about her knowing the spirits. He remembered, when they were both little, Ashfeather could talk for hours about the spirits with Dustbeak, though he wasn’t ever submerged in the conversation like she was. He remembered seeing them talk the night before Boreas and Dustbeak left home. That night he had realized that even if he didn’t like it, they needed each other, and who was he to prevent his son from being happy?

“So we find Ashfeather and ask her for information,” Brightwing stated.

Dustbeak looked uncomfortable, but nodded. They took a few drinks of the oasis and flew the short distance to the edge of the forest.

After all of this, Boreas was home again.

CHAPTER EIGHT

They landed on the grass and walked into the forest. They were home. Winter was approaching, and the grass was covered in fallen leaves. Boreas remembered a few years ago, when Dustbeak had learned to scoop up all the leaves into a huge pile just to jump into it and scatter them everywhere. He had tried to do the same thing with snow once the leaves were gone, but it was a much colder cushion to land on. Boreas laughed to himself and wondered if Dustbeak remembered that.

Once they were deeper in the forest, Boreas began to smell all the familiar scents and see the places he had grown to know by heart. Some feeling washed over him, but he couldn't quite figure out what it was. Joy for finally coming home? Anxiety about finding the spirits?

Maybe a hint of guilt. Guilt for staying put his whole life, just like every other griffin in this forest. This was the only thing he had ever known, and he had been fine with that. Perhaps it wasn't even the guilt of not knowing, but not trying to know. He felt guilty for the entire Golden Forest, teaching that everything outside the forest was bad and anyone that wasn't a griffin was dangerous.

As they walked along the path, Boreas got nervous. Last time they were here Mira and Nightshade were hidden in the mountains, but now they were marching right in. It was sure to cause all sorts of panic among the griffins.

Sure enough, Boreas heard rustling in the branches. Unlike in the Silver Forest, the sounds didn't scare him, even though they were exactly the same. They made him feel at home. He was bothered, though both at the fact that he was being watched by curious and scared griffins, and at the fact that he wasn't scared.

If what Mira said was true and the Golden and Silver forests were the same, then why would he be afraid in the Silver Forest? Had years of cautionary tales really impacted him that much? He thought he was one of the less paranoid griffins, but maybe he was just as fooled by history as the others.

As they walked further, Boreas heard numerous yells and the sounds of running griffins. He remembered when Nightshade had flown over the forest. It had terrified everyone. And now she was getting even closer.

Finally they reached the main clearing, where Boreas's house was, and where everyone usually gathered. It was their best bet at finding the right griffin to help them. As they entered the clearing, it sent a few screams into the air and some griffins ran for cover. Most of them stayed, though, at the sight of Boreas and Dustbeak leading Mira and Nightshade. Boreas stopped in the middle of the clearing and

Dustbeak limped forward to stand beside him, leaning on him slightly for support.

"Don't be afraid," Boreas said.

The griffins just stared.

"We're not here to hurt you," Mira said, stepping forward. A few more griffins turned and ran.

"Boreas, what are you doing?" a voice rose from the crowd. Blacktail stepped forward cautiously.

"Don't be afraid," Boreas repeated. "They won't hurt us."

"He brought the dragon to the forest!" one of the griffins yelled.

"He's working for them!" another spat.

Several more yells erupted from the crowd.

Finally, Dustbeak shouted above them all, "Everyone listen!"

Boreas nodded to Dustbeak gratefully and continued, "This is Mira and Nightshade, everyone. No, they are not griffins. Is that why you fear them? Do you fear the fish that swim in the river, or the birds that chirp in the trees?"

The crowd was quiet, so Boreas kept going.

"We were taught to fear things that were different from us. I was too. And I did, even after I left. But Mira has shown herself as not just a good elf, but a good friend. And it's made me realize that we shouldn't fear elves just because they're different."

"But some of us have been hurt by elves! We know griffins that have been killed by them!" someone shouted.

"And Mira knows elves that have been hurt or killed by griffins," Boreas said.

He heard Mira's voice in his head saying almost that exact sentence. Except when she had said the words, they were directed at him.

He didn't know why it felt urgent for him to make them understand. He still second-guessed Mira sometimes. But no matter how he put it, she was his friend now. And he needed to make sure that no elf was wrongly judged again. And it wasn't just about the elves—it was about the Golden Forest itself. If Boreas could convince the griffins that the outside world wasn't as dangerous as it seemed, the forest would be better off. Maybe the forest could even become a home for more than just griffins. Perhaps the Emerald Woodland could be a reality once again.

Blacktail took another step toward Boreas. "Boreas," he said. "Do you really believe that elves are not dangerous?"

"It's not elves as a whole," Boreas explained. "Yes, I believe that elves as a species are not what we thought they were. But at the same time, that doesn't mean that an elf will never hurt someone or do bad things. And it's the same for griffins. When we were traveling, we met a griffin who almost killed me and Dustbeak. But Mira saved us. So can you really say one species is less violent than the other?"

Blacktail frowned and his eyebrows bent together. He looked at his feet for a moment, then looked back at Boreas and smiled slightly. Blacktail then turned to the crowd.

"I believe Boreas," he said.

Many whispers were passed around the clearing. Finally another griffin stepped out next to Blacktail.

"I believe him as well." It was Vapor, Cattail's father.

Soon almost all the griffins that hadn't run away had stepped forward to join Blacktail. Boreas looked around, proud of himself and his son for venturing beyond the forest, all to stand right here and say this.

Boreas scanned the crowd, realizing he couldn't find the face he had been unconsciously looking for. After several worrying moments, he finally spotted her.

Silverpelt was near the back of the crowd, pushing her way through the griffins trying to get to the front. She spotted Boreas and her eyes lit up as he ran to her. When they reached each other, Boreas tightly wrapped his wings around her. The last time he had seen her, he was flying away into danger. And now he was back, and she was his again.

Dustbeak joined them, leaning against Silverpelt to put pressure off his leg. Boreas didn't know how long it had been when Silverpelt reluctantly pulled away.

"Boreas, what happened?" she asked.

Boreas shook his head. It was too much to explain right now. But Dustbeak stepped back and sat down, beginning the story. By the time he was finished Mira had joined them and Silverpelt was staring at Dustbeak with an unreadable expression. Boreas couldn't tell if she was surprised, terrified, or just in awe. She sat back and shook her head a few times.

"Boreas, I know you want to reunite with your family, but we have to find Ashfeather," Mira said quietly after a few minutes.

Boreas sighed and looked back at Silverpelt. "She's right," he said. "Do you know where she is?"

Silverpelt nodded. "She just flew off to her tree a few minutes before you came. She should still be there, unless she saw your dragon and came back."

"Mira, do you have any more of those leaves?" Dustbeak asked.

He had stood up now and was trying to hold his leg up, but the make-shift cast made it harder because he couldn't bend his knee.

"Sorry, I'm all out," Mira said.

"What kind of herb is it?" Blacktail asked from behind them.

Though Boreas had almost forgotten about them, the griffins were still gathered and all of them were talking quietly in small groups.

"Pensix. Purple flowers, long green leaves," Mira told him.

Blacktail nodded. "That grows all around my home. I'll go grab some."

Mira watched him run into the trees. "As soon as he gets back, we have to look for Ashfeather."

"I'll start asking around," Boreas offered. "Maybe someone else knows something."

Mira and Dustbeak nodded and Boreas started back toward the crowd. Most of the griffins were huddled in small groups, keeping their distance from Nightshade. Boreas didn't blame them. A dragon was in their forest, and even if they did believe Boreas that she wouldn't hurt them, it was still scary.

He started questioning a few of them, though most of the answers were very unhelpful. Everything everyone knew just came from the stories passed down through generations. A griffin named Terrain claimed that his sister had seen the spirits, once, but Terrain refused to give her name.

Once he was sure that no one in this clearing would know anything useful, he went back to his family. Dustbeak was standing more confidently and saying something to Blacktail. When he reached them Mira nodded to Boreas and headed toward Nightshade to mount up.

"Be careful," Silverpelt said when Boreas stood in front of her.

"We'll be all right," Boreas said.

Silverpelt rested her head against Boreas's. He didn't want to leave her again, not ever.

But he had a job to do.

They left the clearing and all the griffins in it behind them and started toward Ashfeather's house. When they got there Dustbeak rushed over to the tree she had made her home in and called her name. There was no response.

"Ashfeather?" Boreas shouted.

"She's not here," Mira stated.

"Come on, we have to look for her," Dustbeak said.

He started limping deeper into the forest and repeating her name.

They searched until the moon was high in the sky. Boreas was exhausted from the days of flying across the desert and everything before that, and the darkness just made him more tired.

"We've been looking for almost three hours," Boreas said. "Let's take a break. We can keep looking in the morning."

"We have to find her," Mira insisted.

"Not tonight," Dustbeak complained.

His eyes were half closed, and he was slowing down.

Mira hesitated. Finally she groaned and said, "Arrrg. Fine. First thing in the morning, though, we're looking for her."

"Why are you in such a hurry?" Boreas asked her.

Ever since they got here it seemed like Mira was on a schedule.

Mira shifted uncomfortably. "I—I just want to find the spirits, all right? It's... best to get to them sooner than later, that's all."

Dustbeak and Boreas shared a suspicious glance, but they didn't pressure the elf. They went back to the clearing, seeing that most of the griffins had dispersed. Boreas and Dustbeak flew up to their tree to spend one more night with Silverpelt since they had the chance. They hesitated to leave Mira, but she insisted she and Nightshade would be fine down on the ground.

In the morning, Boreas woke up before Dustbeak and flew to the ground. Mira and Nightshade were gone, and the dirt had a strange pattern drawn in it. Boreas recognized parts of the scribbles from Mira's map, but he couldn't tell what it was.

Never mind that. She'll come back for me. This just means I have a little more time with Silverpelt.

Boreas stretched his stiff wings and yawned. Then a thought crossed his mind. Since they entered the forest, Boreas had seen no sign of Brightwing. He had forgotten about the old griffin in all the commotion. Where had he gone?

Probably ran off the first chance he got, Boreas thought.

Still, something told him that Brightwing hadn't just left them. There was more to this.

CHAPTER NINE

When Mira returned almost an hour later to find Boreas, Dustbeak, and Silverpelt eating breakfast, she stared in disbelief.

"What are you doing?" she asked. "'I've been waiting for you for *two hours*!"

"How were we supposed to know?" Dustbeak asked, looking up at her.

"I left you a note! Did you not see it?" Mira pointed to the little squiggles in the dirt.

"That's a note? What is it supposed to mean?" Boreas asked.

Mira smacked her forehead and muttered, "Right. You can't read. Come on, Nightshade and I found where Ashfeather went."

"Hey, have you seen Brightwing?" Boreas asked, standing and helping Dustbeak to his feet.

"No, he disappeared right after we left the oasis," Mira said. "Probably ran away as soon as he could."

"I don't know..." Boreas murmured. "Something doesn't feel right."

"Come on, let's go," Mira insisted.

"All right, we're coming," Dustbeak grumbled, walking toward her.

Silverpelt whispered, "Be safe," and watched them go.

Boreas smiled at her as he started to walk away. He felt bad leaving her again when he had just returned, but he would be back soon.

They followed Mira through the forest and across the river. Many of the griffins they passed gave them suspicious looks, but Boreas was pleased to see that only one of them ran away from the elf.

When they reached the opposite end of the forest, Boreas spotted Nightshade standing outside a cave in the mountain. He recognized the cave as the same one they had hid inside on the day they found Brightwing.

"Good job Nightshade," Mira said, patting the dragon on the shoulder as she walked into the cave.

Boreas and Dustbeak followed her inside. Once Boreas's eyes adjusted to the darkness, he saw Ashfeather sitting against the wall. Her white fur seemed dull, like there was a thin layer of dust over it, and the grey of her feathers matched the stone behind her. Dustbeak ran over to her immediately.

"Dustbeak?" Ashfeather sat up, her eyes wide. "Thank the spirits you're all right!"

"What happened? Why are you here?" Dustbeak asked.

"I came here after I saw the dragon enter the forest. I recognized it as the same one from the oasis, and I knew the elf would be with it. I had to—" Ashfeather hesitated. A strange look crossed her face for a heartbeat, then she continued. "I had to get out of there, so I ran here. I was coming to find you this morning but the dragon found me."

"We're not going to hurt you and you know it," Mira spat.

Ashfeather glared at Mira and stepped closer to Dustbeak.

"What are you doing here?" she asked.

"Ashfeather, I know you're scared, but Mira just wants to help," Boreas said.

"I'm not scared," Ashfeather said flatly. "I just want to know what's going on."

"What's 'going on' is we have to find the spirits, and fast," Mira said.

"When did we get in such a hurry?" Dustbeak asked. "You've been acting weird, Mira. What's wrong?"

Mira sighed and looked around, as if looking for an excuse or something else to talk about. Finally she frowned and said, "We're running out of time."

"Why? What's going to happen?" Boreas asked.

"I'm not sure exactly. But something bad is coming, and it's coming soon. We need to find the spirits *soon*, or we may never get the chance," Mira said.

Nightshade entered the cave and lowered her head, making a sound like purring when Mira placed her hand on the dragon's snout. Mira whispered something to her dragon and Nightshade looked at the griffins, growling softly.

"Mira, no more secrets," Dustbeak said. "This has been bothering me for a while now. How do you communicate with Nightshade? If you stop hiding it, maybe she can be more help to us. Maybe she knows something."

"She doesn't know anything I don't," Mira said quietly. "So it won't help. But I guess at this rate we're all going to die anyway, so fine." She paused for a moment to look at Nightshade, then confessed. "When a dragon chooses its partner, their minds connect. We always know where the other is, and we can... talk, in a way. Not with words, but more of thoughts, ideas, or emotions."

They were silent for a moment, then Ashfeather said, "Interesting. But you were right—unhelpful. I want to help, and maybe you would have known that if you didn't trap me in a cave all morning."

"Well, maybe you shouldn't have run away," Mira retorted, placing her hands on her hips.

"So what do you need?" Ashfeather asked. "Obviously I know something, or you think I know something."

"We need to find the spirits," Boreas said.

Ashfeather looked away and clamped her beak shut, saying nothing.

What's so bad about helping us find them? Wouldn't she want to find them? Didn't she say something to Dustbeak once about dedicating her life to them?

"Ashfeather, I know you think they should stay hidden, but you heard Mira. We need to find them," Dustbeak pleaded. "Do you know where they are?"

Ashfeather thought for a moment, then sighed and shrugged. "Well, there are rumors of them hiding at a place called the Skyspire, and others claiming they are across the Scorchwood Valley at Quake Canyon. Or they could also be—"

"Ashfeather, the real place. You know; I can tell. Show us where they are," Mira said.

A chill went down Boreas's spine. Did she really know, all this time? They flew halfway across Arcenti, and she knew where they were?

Ashfeather was quiet for several seconds. Then her tail twitched and she raised her head.

"Protect at all costs." She sounded like she was reciting a rule, like a hatchling repeating a rule to her parents.

"What?" Dustbeak asked, putting a wing over her. "Ash, what are you talking about?"

Ashfeather stood up, her eyes wild. "I'm sorry," she whispered to Dustbeak.

"Sorry for what? Ashfeather, what are you doing?" Boreas asked, stepping towards her.

Ashfeather closed her eyes and flicked her tail again. Then, suddenly, she rolled away from Dustbeak, kicking his injured leg out from under him before springing to her feet and darting toward Boreas. He didn't have time to react before he was on the ground. She was just a white and grey blur as she hurdled over Mira's head. Ashfeather was almost out of the cave when Nightshade leapt out in front of her and swatted her to the ground, pinning her down.

"Let me go!" Ashfeather yelled, clawing at Nightshade's talons.

It was no use—Nightshade's thick green scales protected her against Ashfeather's claws.

"Wow. You are a *terrible* liar," Mira stated, crouching next to the flailing griffin. "So where are they?"

"I'll never tell you," Ashfeather hissed, her tail lashing.

Boreas helped Dustbeak to his feet, wincing at the way Dustbeak's face contorted with pain, and they walked over to her. Boreas didn't know what to say. They had been searching for the answer for so long, and now it was right in front of them. But they couldn't reach it.

"Ashfeather, please," Dustbeak begged. "If you know where they are, you have to tell us."

Ashfeather said nothing, but she stopped struggling and stared blankly at Dustbeak.

"Ashfeather, we're all going to die if you don't give us a location right now," Mira threatened.

"I'm not afraid of you," Ashfeather hissed.

"But you should be afraid of shades," Mira pointed out. "And if you don't help us find the spirits, then the world will be overrun with them before the next full moon."

"Ashfeather, please," Boreas said. "We need to find them."

Ashfeather was still quiet. Boreas realized that no matter what they tried, she wouldn't give up the location.

Then something strange happened.

Ashfeather relaxed and looked up at them with wide eyes. "I'll tell you," she whispered. She looked far away, not completely focused.

"I—okay, great," Mira said slowly. "Where are they?"

"Follow me," Ashfeather said.

Mira nodded to Nightshade and the dragon lifted her claws to release Ashfeather. She walked slowly out of the cave and towards the river.

"This is a trap," Mira muttered.

"She wouldn't do that," Dustbeak hissed back.

"We don't know that," Boreas worried. "I mean, she knows where the spirits are hiding. Not even you guessed that. She's unpredictable. I haven't trusted her since the day you met her."

"So, say it is a trap—which it will be, what do we do?" Mira asked.

"I guess we see where she's taking us, and if there are any red flags we get out of there as soon as possible," Boreas suggested.

Mira shook her head. "This whole thing is a red flag. We need leverage, something to keep her from hurting us. If she really is on the spirits' side, who knows what kind of power she could have."

"If it *is* a trap, I can be your leverage. She doesn't want to hurt me," Dustbeak offered.

Mira shook her head. "She's unpredictable right now. You can't say with complete certainty that she won't hurt you."

"She won't," Dustbeak insisted.

"I'm not going to hurt any of you," Ashfeather said quietly.

Dustbeak gave Mira a pointed look, but Mira didn't see it. She was staring at Ashfeather, trying to figure her out. The white griffin said nothing else as they crossed the river and continued walking.

"Where are we going?" Boreas asked.

He was beginning to get nervous as they walked on. Could they really trust her? One moment she's attacking them, and the next she agrees to take them with no terms, not even an explanation? And now she wasn't telling them anything. Dustbeak was certain that her intentions were pure, or maybe he just really wanted to believe that, but Boreas wasn't so sure.

The forest suddenly went dark, and Boreas looked up to see a blanket of clouds blocking the sun. Mira and Dustbeak glanced up as well, but Ashfeather didn't seem to notice.

They reached the clearing soon after. Boreas looked at his tree and saw that Silverpelt was gone, probably out hunting or with one of her friends. Ashfeather led them to the opposite end and a couple steps into the trees, then stopped.

"Are we here?" Mira asked immediately.

Ashfeather nodded slightly and flicked her wing towards a huge oak tree.

"So this is it? This is where they're hiding?" Dustbeak asked, getting closer to Ashfeather than Boreas was comfortable with.

"Yes," Ashfeather said.

"All right, where's the trap? I've passed this tree a hundred times, there's no spirits in it. What did you set up? Do you have friends or something coming to ambush us?" Boreas asked, stepping toward her.

This griffin had been endangering his family long enough by getting close to Dustbeak. And before he left on this crazy mission, he had actually begun to trust her. Boreas flicked his tail and gestured for Dustbeak to stand beside him. Dustbeak took a small step away from Ashfeather, but didn't walk towards his father. Nightshade sniffed the air and growled quietly.

"What is it, girl?" Mira whispered to her dragon, petting her snout.

Nightshade looked at Mira for a few seconds, then stood straighter and walked towards the tree.

"She doesn't think it's a trap," Mira said.

"I told you, this is where they are," Ashfeather insisted. "I can't—"

She paused and stared at the ground for several seconds.

"Are you sure—" she whispered under her breath, then stopped and nodded a heartbeat later. "Okay, I'll explain everything to you."

Mira looked at her suspiciously and Boreas glanced around the forest, looking for whoever she had just talked to. He saw no one and heard nothing. So who was she whispering to?

"Ashfeather, you can tell me anything," Dustbeak said encouragingly.

Ashfeather sighed and began. "I can't believe, after all these years, I'm about to give up the most important secret in the world."

"Go on," Mira said warily.

Ashfeather sighed again. "Nineteen years ago, almost to this day, I was chosen for one of the most important things I could imagine."

She stopped and closed her eyes for a few seconds before taking a deep breath and continuing, "I am a guardian of the spirits."

Boreas took a moment to process that. But he couldn't wrap his head around what she had said. All he could do was stare at her.

"When I was chosen, to protect my identity and make sure I would protect them for a long time to come, the spirits changed my appearance. They... reset my life, in a way. They made me look like a hatchling again in other creatures' eyes, so I would appear to have a regular life. I looked like I was growing up and changing, though I've stayed the same age. I played the part of a normal, unnoticeable griffin named Windfur. And this way I could protect the spirits for as long as they needed me, until I thought it was best to choose a new guardian. My mind stayed inside the tree, though. I could see everything that was happening outside but I couldn't feel anything a normal griffin would. It was like—controlling a puppet, in a way."

Ashfeather looked at each of them, resting her gaze on Dustbeak for a split second before looking at her talons.

"Everything was fine until a few years after I was chosen, when I met Dustbeak. The spirits and I knew I wouldn't be able to stay away from him, so they changed me again—Windfur died, and I moved further from the other griffins, to the edge of the forest. But Dustbeak came back into my life, even closer this time. I knew I couldn't just change again, so I tried to limit myself but it got out of hand. Finally the spirits agreed to let me stay as Ashfeather, to actually live in the Golden Forest with other griffins, and protect the tree from the outside. I can't see what's happening in the world anymore, but I can feel things. I was supposed to keep the secret for eternity, but then you three came along, and the spirits told me to let you find them."

"All this time..." Dustbeak trailed off.

Boreas didn't know what to think. He remembered Windfur—she had lived just outside the clearing. Dustbeak had only known her for a few weeks before she died, and Boreas was pretty sure he didn't even remember her. Everyone thought she had drowned in the river, and her body had even been found in the sand. Now that he thought about it, he couldn't remember ever meeting her parents.

Because they don't exist. Her life is all a lie.

She's the guardian of the spirits. Should I be mad, because she tricked us? Fooled my son? Should I apologize for not trusting her, even though she really was hiding something?

Mira and Nightshade stared in awe at Ashfeather. Boreas could tell that the elf didn't know what to think either.

Finally Dustbeak broke the silence.

"What do you really look like?" he asked quietly, like he was afraid to talk too loud. "Who are you, really?"

Ashfeather sighed and closed her eyes again. A soft golden light surrounded her, getting brighter. Within a few seconds Boreas had to look away. Then the light vanished, and standing in Ashfeather's place was a tall griffin with light grey fur and rose-gold feathers. Her back legs and tail were white.

"My name is Ruby," she said.

Dustbeak backed away from her and stood next to Boreas. "So you've been lying to us, for all these years?"

Ruby stepped toward him. "Dustbeak it's not like that—"

"I don't want your excuses!" Dustbeak roared. "I thought we were friends! I thought you said no lies! I thought—" He looked at Ruby, then turned his head away from her. "I thought we had something."

"Dustbeak—"

"Stop! How do I know *this* is even you? You're fake, and everything you've ever said to me is fake. Ashfeather isn't real. *You're* not real!" Dustbeak cried.

"Dustbeak, I'm real! Ashfeather may not be my name and that may not have been my fur, but I am real, our *experiences* are real!" Ruby argued desperately.

"Ash—*Ruby*," Boreas caught himself. "Maybe it's best if you give all of us a minute."

Ruby opened her mouth to complain, but saw Boreas's stern look and nodded, quietly walking into the underbrush.

"Wow," Mira whispered as soon as she was gone. "I guess we found our guard." To herself she added under her breath, "I *knew* I felt something off her when we first met."

"Yeah, you think?" Dustbeak snapped. "And it just happened to be one of the only griffins I care for."

"Easy Dustbeak," Boreas said. "We're all surprised."

Dustbeak glared at Boreas and he scolded himself in his head. That was probably the wrong thing to say.

"So, what do we do now?" Boreas asked, trying to take the subject off Ruby.

"We ask her to talk to the spirits," Mira said. "Ask them to help us. We need to do it fast—whatever's coming is getting close. Nightshade can feel something nearby, something bad. I can sense it too."

"Okay, so we ask her to talk to the spirits for us. What happens if they say no?" Dustbeak asks.

"They better not. If they say no we have no backup. We did all this for nothing. And, you know, the world might end," Mira said.

"And if they say yes?" Boreas asked. "What do we do then? Just sit back and watch them?"

Mira shrugged. "I don't know everything, you guys! But in theory, they'll know what to do."

Dustbeak turned around and stepped toward where Ruby had disappeared.

"A—Ruby," he called, almost calling her the wrong name. "Come back."

A few seconds later she pushed through the bushes and looked at him awkwardly. "You know, you can call me Ashfeather if you want. I... kind of got used to it."

"Well it would be a lot easier if you *were* Ashfeather," Dustbeak said begrudgingly.

"I can be," Ruby whispered. "I can change back if you want me to."

"Do whatever you want, I don't care. But can you help us?" Dustbeak asked, turning away.

Ruby nodded and walked over to Boreas and Mira, keeping her head angled down.

"What do you need?" she asked. "I'm supposed to help with anything you ask."

"We need you to talk to the spirits for us," Mira said. "Can you do that?"

Ruby nodded and was about to say something but Mira cut her off. "We need to ask them to help us. The dark spirit is growing stronger by the second and overtaking more lives by the day. They need to stop it, just like they did before."

Ruby nodded again and closed her eyes. She grew tense, and they all waited. Not even the birds in the trees made a noise. The whole forest was waiting.

Then Ruby let out a long breath and opened her eyes.

"Well?" Mira pressured.

Ruby said nothing, just looked at the tree with an unreadable expression and gulped.

The bark of the tree suddenly shifted, then slithered away from the middle of the trunk. One by one each piece retreated until there was a wide circle of smooth wood on the tree.

The wood shimmered, then slowly vanished. In its place was a bright hole filled with light.

And the spirits emerged.

CHAPTER TEN

Boreas was breathless. The spirits were like nothing he ever could have imagined. Each of them took a different astonishing form, like the ones on the carving but more majestic and unbelievable. Once they all came out of the tree, one of them stepped forward to greet their audience.

The spirit that stepped toward them had a build similar to a tiger, but with a long, prehensile tail and short horns between its ears. Its fur looked like a hundred different shades of dark blue and purple, like it was made of the deepest part of the oceans and the skies. Its eyes were multicolored and looked like they had reflections of the moon in them.

"Greetings," the spirit said, and immediately Mira dropped to one knee in a bow.

Boreas wondered if he should do the same when Ruby bowed her head and spread her wings. He followed her position and Dustbeak caught on as well.

"We do not have time for customary gestures," another spirit whispered.

Their voices were soft and light, but dark and solemn at the same time, and it was tricking Boreas's ears. This spirit looked like a large red snake with two golden stripes down either side of its body. Like the tiger, its scales were an intriguing mix of every shade of red Boreas had seen and more. It slithered up next to the tiger, keeping its long neck and head suspended off the ground. Mira rose to her feet and the griffins slowly followed suit.

The snake looked at Mira with its piercing yellow eyes until she looked down, away from it. Then it said in its whispery voice, "I see our message has found you. Yet you come without the others. Why?"

"No, they did not receive the message," the tiger hissed. "The guardian we sent has been overtaken by Skoti. They only saw the map."

"Message?" Mira asked quietly.

Boreas admired the courage it took to say that; he felt like he was interrupting these divine creatures by simply breathing.

The snake looked at her again and started to explain. "The day I left our hideout to record Skoti's progress, I knew it would not be long until it grew too strong. So we sent one of our guardians to find the right creature to help us, and to find the others. He found you, born with part of me inside, but you were far too young. So the guardian waited for you in that cave. He knew you would come looking eventually, and if not then your dragon would, in time, take you there. But our guardian could not resist Skoti for long, and he too was lost to the darkness."

"Who is Skoti?" Dustbeak asked after a moment.

"The dark spirit," Ruby whispered. "It overtook the guardian and turned it into a shade."

"What was the message? I'm sure we can still follow through," Mira suggested.

Both the spirits shook their heads. "It is too late now. Skoti is growing more powerful, and it seeks revenge. If we are to save your world, we cannot allow it to reach us," the snake said.

The tiger continued. "The message you were supposed to receive would have told you to find the other spirits. The water, land, and sky, and any clues we had to where they are hidden. But now it is too late. We have no time to send you on another adventure. You must stay here with us."

"We can do it," Boreas said.

Suddenly he wanted nothing more than to find the others and bring them back. It was the only way he could truly protect his family.

Another spirit joined the conversation, this one a large golden-colored eagle that's wings were producing some sort of ora that made it look like it was glowing or standing in fire.

"There are others that will find them," the eagle said. "But it will not be you, and it may take several years."

"We don't have that kind of time," Mira insisted. "The dark spirit—Skoti—it's coming."

"We are well aware. But with strong guardians, we will be safe, and we can save your world when the time comes," the snake said.

"So, what do we do?" Dustbeak asked. "Just wait for that to happen?"

"Why can't it be us?" Mira chimed in.

"You will stay with us, and become guardians. Your minds are strong, stronger than we have seen in a long time. You are what we need," the tiger explained calmly.

"What?" Boreas exclaimed. *Become a guardian? Protect the spirits? Should I be honored, or afraid?*

"Unless, that is, you do not wish for that to be arranged," the eagle said, noticing their disbelief.

"Can we... uh, can we have a moment to talk about it?" Dustbeak asked awkwardly.

The spirits nodded and the three of them backed up and formed a little circle to talk. Nightshade stuck her head in as well and grunted.

"She thinks we should do it," Mira translated.

"What about you?" Boreas asked. "What do you think?"

Mira frowned and furrowed her brow. Finally she answered, "I don't know what to think. I mean, being a spirit guardian... that's serious. Who wouldn't accept that offer? It's something everyone dreams about back home."

"But...?" Boreas asked.

Mira sighed. "But we wouldn't know what was happening outside the forest. I mean, I've been all over the world, and the longest I've ever stayed in one place is a few months. I don't know what it's like to stay put."

"I can say from experience, it's not as glamorous as traveling," Dustbeak said after a moment. "I mean, I've been here my whole life, and then everything is uprooted and we get to fly halfway across Arcenti. It was amazing... but I agree with Nightshade. I think we should accept it."

"Boreas?" Mira asked, turning to him.

Boreas was silent for a long time. Could he really just give up his life, say goodbye to everyone he knew? He would still be in the forest, but if it was like Ruby's life, he would have to give up Silverpelt.

Or maybe he wouldn't have to. Ruby still managed to have Dustbeak, even though she had to fake her own death to get him. Could he choose the spirits and still have his family?

It was a long time before he answered. But finally, after wearing himself down arguing in his mind, he decided.

"I'm with Dustbeak," he said at last. "I think we should do it."

Mira and Dustbeak stared at him for a few seconds, then Mira shook her head and said, "All right, then. I'm in."

Dustbeak nodded and they turned back to the spirits. The sight of them still dazzled Boreas. Now the rest had formed a line with the first three. He saw some spirits that looked like strangely colored animals, and others that couldn't be compared to anything ordinary.

"Have you made your decision?" the tiger asked.

The three of them exchanged a nervous look. Then Mira took a step forward and said, "Yes. We would be honored to be guardians of the spirits."

The tiger nodded to them and the snake said, "You should know that this choice will change you forever. Even once you return to your lives, nothing will be the same."

The three of them nodded, and the snake dipped its head.

"Your change will be different from others you have heard of," the tiger began, glancing at Ruby. "You will guard from the inside, not the outside. There will be no appearance changes necessary, but you will not be seen by anyone until Nera, Gano, and Ouran—the others—have been retrieved."

"So we won't be able to live in the Golden Forest anymore? Will we be able to come back?" Boreas asked.

The tiger nodded slowly. "We see all that happens, so you will not be completely cut off. But you will not return until Skoti has been overpowered."

Can I really give up my life for this? Can I give up Silverpelt?

Boreas didn't say anything. Instead he nodded and looked back up at the spirits. He believed he was ready. He could do it. *This is the only way to truly protect her.*

"Fengara, we must hurry. There are shades near," the snake whispered to the tiger.

Fengara nodded and continued. "In order to enter our land, you must become part of everything around you, including each other. Once you enter, your minds will join for a short time—a few seconds for us, but it will seem longer for you. You will not know what is happening, who you are, or know anything that you know now. But this will only last for a moment, and then you will enter."

The three of them looked at each other with one last bit of hesitation. Boreas admitted to himself that he was scared. No, he was terrified. He was about to leave everything he had known and venture into the unexplainable.

But he didn't turn back. For once in his life, fear didn't deter him.

Nightshade walked up behind them and grunted. Fengara shook its head. "No, dragon. I'm afraid your protection is needed here, with Ruby. Don't worry. You will see your friend again."

Nightshade snorted hot air out of her nose and bent down to nuzzle Mira.

"You mean she can't come?" Mira asked sadly.

Fengara shook its head again. Mira sighed and wrapped her arms around Nightshade's neck.

"I'll see you soon, girl," she whispered.

Nightshade made a long, sad moaning sound and Mira whispered something Boreas couldn't hear. The dragon responded with a sad growl.

"I know. I don't want to leave you either. But I'll see you again. You be good to the griffins, all right?"

Nightshade pushed her head into Mira one last time, then pulled away and took a step back to watch them leave.

"We're ready," Mira said. Boreas thought he saw her wipe her eyes quickly as she turned around. "Let's do this."

Boreas looked at Dustbeak, who was looking around the forest with wide eyes, trying to soak everything in.

"Dad, I'm scared. What if we never see mom again?" Dustbeak asked.

"It'll be all right," Boreas whispered to his son. He put a wing over Dustbeak's back and hugged him close. "But if you don't want to go, you don't have to. You should stay behind with your mom and Ruby."

Dustbeak looked up at him for a second, then squeezed his eyes closed and shook his head. "No. I want to do this. I need to. We need to do it together."

"Prepare yourselves," the eagle said.

It spread its wings, letting rays of light engulf the area like the sun just came out, then walked back into the tree. The others followed it slowly, all disappearing into the light, until only Fengara was left.

"Come," the moon spirit said. It turned around and started toward the Great Oak.

"Here we go," Mira murmured under her breath.

They followed Fengara toward the tree. It looked back at them, then stepped through and disappeared. The three of them paused for a moment, hesitant. Then Mira looked back at Nightshade one last time, and stepped into the light. Dustbeak and Boreas looked at each other, then stepped in at the same time.

~~~

Mira looked at the dragon egg with wonder. A strange elf that lived near the Fangrocks had just given it to her and said that it was now her duty to care for it. It would hatch in three days, and then it would choose her, as his dragon had chosen him when he was young.

The egg was dark green and felt warm when she picked it up. She had to set it right back down, however, because the egg was almost as big as her and very heavy.

"Mira, let me carry it inside for you. Calun will help you build a nest for it, so the dragon will be comfortable when it hatches."

Mira looked up at Elek, her father, and handed him the egg. He took it inside their small hut and she followed him, keeping a close eye on the egg. She already felt responsible for it, like the dragon inside had already chosen her. Calun told his dragon, a huge beast with orange scales, to wait outside as he followed them in.

"What if it doesn't like me?" Mira worried aloud. "A lot of the other kids don't. What if the dragon doesn't?"
~~~

"Mira, it has no reason not to like you. You will be the perfect partner for this dragon, and you will care for each other," Calun assured her.

That night, Mira spent hours touching up on the nest Calun had helped her build. She lined it with one of the quilts from her bed, then added some soft leaves. She wanted everything to be perfect for the dragonling.

Three days passed, and like Calun had said, the egg hatched. From it came a beautiful dragonling with dark green scales, blue spines, and floppy wings that it could not yet lift.

"Hello there," Mira said as it examined its nest.

The dragonling turned around and looked up at her with big, yellow-green eyes.

"Let her come to you," Mira's mother, Anali, said quietly from the doorway. She and Elek were trying to give her and the dragon space, but they couldn't help but watch.

The small scaly creature sniffed the nest, then hooked her little claws into the blanket to balance herself while she poked her head over the edge. She looked at Mira again, and their eyes locked. Mira felt a connection to the dragonling already, like there was nothing in all of Arcenti that could separate them.

Suddenly something clicked in her mind, and she felt intense curiosity and wonder. Then surprise, followed shortly after by joy. The dragonling closed her eyes and let out a tiny, high-pitched roar. Mira smiled and laughed a little. This was more amazing than anything she could have imagined.

"What will you name her?" Elek asked.

"Dad, I've never been good with coming up with names," Mira said. "What if she doesn't like the name I choose?"

"I'm sure you can find a perfect one," Anali encouraged her. "Just try. See if she likes any."

Mira thought hard. What could she name this dragonling? After much consideration, she decided to name her after a plant because of her green scales. She began listing plants she knew in her head.

Snakeroot, ivy, vine, hemlock, nightshade, rosemary, cactus...

At one of the thoughts, the dragonling made a chirping noise.

"Which one?" Mira asked her.

The dragonling tilted her head and Mira felt a pull in her mind. She went back over the list, slower this time, and felt a click at one of the names.

Nightshade.

"Nightshade," Mira repeated out loud. "You like that one?"

Nightshade opened her flimsy wings and roared another one of her little baby roars. Mira smiled and reached down to pick up Nightshade. The dragonling scrambled into her arms and pressed herself against Mira, her scales surprisingly warm despite the cold, winter night.

"We'll be together forever," Mira whispered, and she felt Nightshade agree. "Nothing can separate us, ever."

~~~

Dustbeak peered through the leaves around him. He was sitting on a branch, high above the ground. It was warmer today than it had been, which meant that spring was on the verge of ending and summer was coming. The leaves were thick and green, so he was well hidden.

"Ready or not, I'm coming!" Ashfeather's voice rang through the forest below him.

He crouched lower, pushing himself against the branch. After a minute of silence, he spotted his friend wandering below the treetops. Her white fur reflected the sunlight that filtered through the leaves. Dustbeak saw it as a perfect opportunity to pounce, but it would mean losing the game. He restrained himself, but only because of a bet he and Brownclaw had made about who would be found first.

Ashfeather looked up and Dustbeak tensed, but the trees hid him well enough and she moved on.

Later that day, the three friends were walking on the path, laughing.

"I won, I won, *I* won!" Dustbeak bragged, bumping Brownclaw's side.

Brownclaw smirked and crouched low, lashing his tail. Dustbeak raised his talon to hit him playfully, but Brownclaw pounced before he had the chance and tackled Dustbeak to the ground.
~~~

"Can't you two go three minutes without arguing or fighting?" Ashfeather asked as they rolled through the dirt.

Dustbeak laughed and pinned Brownclaw below him, smirking at his friend for a few dramatic seconds before looking up at Ashfeather.

"Only if I win," he joked. Ashfeather rolled her eyes and Brownclaw kicked Dustbeak's leg, making him lose his balance and fall onto the path.

"Ha! Never turn your back on an enemy," Brownclaw recited, boasting what his older brother had taught him.

The three friends went on walking down the path, laughing and playing until they got home.

"See you tomorrow!" Dustbeak called as Ashfeather ran home. Brownclaw gave him one last swipe, which he dodged, before laughing and running to his own home.

"Dustbeak, dinner time!" Boreas called from in the tree.

"Coming!" Dustbeak responded, flying up to the entrance.

He walked in and saw his parents waiting for him with a pile of fish—one of his favorites. He smiled at them and sat down close to Silverpelt, the feathers on her wing tickling him and she bent down to pick a leaf off his head. Boreas leaned over to nudge him gently, and he put his head against his dad's.

Nothing ever needs to change, he thought. We can stay like this forever.

~~~

Boreas looked out over the Scorchwood Valley, the breeze ruffling his feathers. *One day I'll leave*, he thought. *I'll go out into the world and explore and meet all kinds of new friends! And when I come back, everyone will envy me because I was brave enough to leave.*

"What are you looking at, Boreas?"

Boreas turned around and saw a tan griffin with white feathers walking towards him. Boreas had always thought that they could be related from how similar they looked.

Boreas smiled at him. "Hi, Earthquake."

Earthquake sat down next to Boreas and looked around. "What are you doing out here?"

"Oh, nothing. Just looking at the valley," Boreas said.

He knew it was no use to try and explain it to Earthquake. He had tried before, but his friend just didn't understand his desire to leave. Everything they needed was here in the Golden Forest, according to Earthquake. And everyone else for that matter.

"Hey, how about we go hunting?" Earthquake suggested. "I'm starving."

Boreas smiled and said, "Sure. Race you to the river!"

"Oh, you're on!" Earthquake shouted eagerly.

He took off and disappeared into the forest.

Boreas bounded after him, sneaking one last glance at the Scorchwood Valley before chasing his friend into the woods.
~~~

They ran all the way to the river, Boreas splashing in just before Earthquake.

"Dang it!" Earthquake yelled, stomping his talon in the water and splashing Boreas.

"Ha ha! Third time this week, thank you," Boreas laughed.

"Yeah, yeah, don't get your tail in a knot," Earthquake grumbled.

"Come on! I think I smell a rabbit nearby!" Boreas turned and ran out of the river towards the scent.

Once they found the rabbit, Boreas crouched into a bush and waited for his moment. Earthquake crept up behind him and watched the rabbit sniff the air and carefully dig through the grass for food.

"Three..." Boreas counted under his breath.

"Two..." Earthquake continued, reeling himself in for a pounce.

But right when Boreas was supposed to say, 'One', the rabbit looked behind it, saw something, and bounced away before they could react.

"Arg! Come on!" Earthquake complained, standing up and looking for whatever had startled the rabbit. "We were in such a good position!"

"Earthquake!" they heard someone yelling. "Boreas! Come quickly!"

The two friends looked at each other, then sprinted towards whoever was calling them. It was one of Earthquake's friends, and he started running when he saw them. They arrived back near the river, where a few other griffins were gathering.

"What's going on?" Boreas asked.

"Boreas! Over here!" He turned and saw Rainwing, his mother, standing to the side of the crowd.

Boreas walked over to her and looked at her questioningly. Her silvery grey fur was soft and comforting. He could tell she had just been preening it, which she often did when she was worried.

"They found someone in the river," Rainwing explained. Her voice was nervous and quiet.

"So... what's the big deal?" Boreas asked, leaning against her and watching the other griffins worriedly.

"They—they had to pull him out of the water, Boreas. He may be hurt," Rainwing said.

"Is it true?" someone asked from behind them. Boreas saw his dad, Greywing, coming up behind them.

"Watch Boreas," Rainwing whispered to him. Greywing nodded, something passing between them, and took Boreas under his wing. Rainwing started pushing her way through the crowd.

"Who fell in the river, dad?" Boreas asked, looking up at Greywing. He had brown fur and grey wings, hence his name. "Was it someone we know?"

"I don't know," Greywing said, straining his neck to look over the other griffins. "But it's going to be okay. We'll figure it out."

Suddenly there was a loud wail from the other side of the crowd. Everyone fell silent and Greywing became stiff.

A few seconds later Rainwing came back, the other griffins moving out of her way and clearing a path.

"Mom, what's wrong?" Boreas asked, seeing her face.

She looked far away and sad. He didn't understand.

"Rainwing, was it... is what they said..." Greywing trailed off.

Rainwing looked up at him. Boreas saw tears beginning to well up in her eyes. She nodded.

Greywing sucked in a shaky breath and whispered, "No... no... he didn't—no..."

"What's wrong?" Boreas asked.

He couldn't figure out why everyone was so quiet and sad-looking.

"Boreas... it was Branch," Rainwing said after a moment.

"What?" Boreas asked.

Branch was his older brother. They got along fine, but recently Branch had started hanging out with other friends instead of his little brother. Boreas was fine with that, though, because he had his own friends too. But he and Branch still talked often and shared their dreams of adventure outside the forest. Branch was the one who had first sparked Boreas's interest in the outside world.

"Branch fell in the river," Greywing explained quietly. "And—and he couldn't get out in time."

"In time for what?" Boreas asked, still not catching on. "Did he get hurt? Is that why everyone is here, because he hit his head or something?"

"Boreas..." Rainwing tried. He could see pain in her eyes, and she was trying to keep her voice steady, but it was shaking. "He did get hurt. But not the kind of hurt you think..."

Suddenly it clicked for Boreas. Even without his parents telling him, he knew now.

His brother was dead.

"No..." Boreas whispered, his voice catching in his throat.

"Boreas—" Greywing tried tucking Boreas closer under his wing.

"No!" Boreas yelled. He turned and ran as fast as he could.

He's gone. Branch is gone. I'll never see him again.

Boreas ran until his chest ached. He didn't know where he was going, only that he had to run.

Later that night his parents found him huddled inside a hollow tree, crying quietly to himself.

"I'm okay," he whispered when his mom tried to comfort him.

He stood up and started walking home with them.

Boreas decided two things that night.

One: he had to stay. He couldn't leave the Golden Forest if he wanted to have his family. He could stay and be happy with his parents, and maybe someday have his own little family.

And two: he would never fail to protect someone again.

Before he went to sleep that night, he walked out to the river and looked in. It was so calm and clean. It didn't look like a river that had just taken a life.

Boreas picked up a smooth river stone, about the size of his talon. It was light grey and sparkled in the moonlight. He ran his claw over it, then took it home. At the door to his home, which was a small shelter made of branches and leaves, tied with vines and around the base of a tree, he set the stone down. With his claw he traced a deep line in the rock.

"What are you doing?" Rainwing asked, coming out of the house. "It's late. You should be in bed."

"I will now. It's Branch's rock," Boreas said. He didn't explain, only left the rock there and went inside.

He remembered when Branch had taught him how to carve things into rocks like small patterns or dots. It was one of their favorite things to do together. And now Branch could have his rock, and Boreas felt a little bit better.

He promised himself he would never let down his family. He would never speak of Branch to anyone, never let them know what happened today, not even his closest friends. And he would protect everyone he loved with his life.

~~~

Boreas let out his breath. He blinked a few times, remembering where he was. Standing in the forest with Dustbeak and Mira, about to walk into a bright light with the spirits. They all had one foot inside the tree.
~~~

Dustbeak and Mira looked at each other with wide eyes.

"That was..." Dustbeak trailed off.

"It really felt like we were there," Mira said quietly.

"We were sharing memories," Boreas said.

"Yeah but it didn't feel like *my* memory, or even a memory at all. It was like we were living through it," Dustbeak said, shaking his head.

"And I felt everything, knew everything, that the memory held," Mira said.

Boreas looked back at the forest. "I understand now. We're connected."

A long moment passed before Mira broke the silence. "We better go."

Dustbeak nodded and Boreas looked at each of them. "Let's go guard the spirits," he agreed.

Dustbeak smiled at him and pressed his head against Boreas's chest. Then he took a deep breath and stepped further into the light, disappearing into the brightness.

"See you on the other side," Mira said.

She followed Dustbeak.

Boreas looked back at the forest one more time. He saw the trees around him, Ruby and Nightshade sitting quietly a few yards away. He heard the river rushing not too far away. The clouds parted momentarily, and Boreas heard a call. Silverpelt walked into view. Their eyes met and she froze.

They didn't say a word, didn't move. It seemed like the whole world stood still.

Silverpelt dipped her head in understanding, but he heard her whisper, "I know you have to go. But you'll never really be gone."

"This isn't goodbye," Boreas whispered quietly. "I'm not ready for that. We'll see each other again."

Silverpelt's eyes lifted to his, and she nodded.

He knew it could be years before he got to hold her in his wings again.

But he was ready. Knowing what he knew now about the spirits, and about Dustbeak and Mira, he was ready to do everything he could to protect the spirits; protect his home. With his help, they would return again when the world was ready. When the last three spirits came, he could come back.

Boreas had never liked change. He never liked saying goodbye, and he never liked things he didn't understand.

But with everything that had happened to him recently, he was ready. His life had changed forever, and he was okay with it.

Boreas closed his eyes and stepped through the light.

EPILOGUE

Brightwing watched the others land in the forest, but he held back, hovering just behind them. Boreas and Dustbeak seemed too eager to notice his hesitance, and the elf was deep in her own thoughts.

The perfect chance to slip away. The voice slithered into his mind.

Why would he want to sneak away? They were close to finding the spirits. The only reason he had agreed to this was because of the hope that they could rid him of the voice.

Brightwing hovered in the air and watched as they disappeared under the trees. This voice had been with him for a long time now, and since they had begun this journey he had been having trouble deciphering whether each thought was his own or the mysterious voice.

He stayed in the air, arguing with himself. They were so close to finding the spirits, and then maybe his life could go back to normal. The closer he got to the forest, he felt something else inside him grow more powerful. He felt the sun spirit within him constantly, and he had tried so hard to bring it out, but something—he assumed the voice—was keeping it at bay, though he had no idea where it was coming from.

Go, the voice whispered.

He didn't want to listen. He knew this wasn't his mind. It was something else trying to control him, trying to keep him away from the spirits. But what? This was a question he had asked himself a thousand times.

Now is your chance. The voice grew louder. *Go!* It repeated, over and over until finally Brightwing gave in.

He took one last look at the Golden Forest, at his home, before turning and flying south. The sun was just beginning to set, so he would stop in the Silver Forest to sleep.

Where do I go once I'm there? Brightwing wondered.

He landed in the Silver Forest after the sun had completely set and the moon was climbing the sky. He looked around for anything special about this spot, which the voice had guided him toward. Finding nothing, he found a slightly sheltered place next to a tree with low-hanging branches and curled up to sleep for the night, wishing he was home.

Maybe in the morning it will be gone, he hoped. He wished the same thing every night, but every morning the voice was still there.

He dipped into an uneasy sleep, shadows dancing in the corners of his vision.

In the morning, Brightwing woke up feeling cold. *Winter can't have come yet*, he thought. *The trees still have plenty of leaves to lose.*

He got up and wandered around the area. He didn't know what he was waiting for, or why he was even here. But the voice had said nothing since he arrived, so he must be in the right place. Or maybe it just wanted him away from Boreas, Dustbeak, and Mira.

Maybe I should have fought it. Maybe if I had pushed the voice away from the beginning, it wouldn't have grown so loud. Maybe it wouldn't have taken control.

Brightwing sighed and continued on, keeping his eyes on his feet. He debated returning to the elf village, as he could hear faint sounds of a community coming from nearby, but decided against it and kept walking. He didn't know where he was going or why, but he kept searching. What he was searching for, he didn't know.

Brightwing was still deep in thought when he tripped over a stone and tumbled to the ground. The land below him had begun to tilt down, so he started rolling, head over tail, downhill.

"Ahhh!" Brightwing yelped, trying to dig his claws into the dirt.

It was too soft and just came away with his talons.

In a few seconds, he stopped falling and plunged into a river. The water soaked his fur and the cold penetrated his skin. Brightwing lifted his head, sputtering and blinking water out of his eyes.

"Okay, okay, I'll pay more attention," Brightwing grumbled to himself.

He couldn't help but feel the voice had something to do with this. Though, he had started to blame almost everything on the voice, so it was possible that he was just clumsy. He didn't admit it to himself.

Suddenly there was a quiet laughter coming from in front of him. Brightwing looked up and saw a young elf sitting on a rock by the side of the river. She was grinning and trying to hold in her laugh.

"What are you looking at?" Brightwing growled, standing up and shaking to get some of the water off.

"Nothing," the elf sang cheerfully. "Everyone falls into the river every now and then."

She had light brown hair that was tied up with a vine and her eyes were huge and bright green. Brightwing was surprised she wasn't scared of him; according to Mira, most elves were taught to fear griffins.

"Yeah, yeah," Brightwing muttered.

You're going to let her mock you like that? Pathetic! The voice hissed.

Shut up, Brightwing told it. *You're not the boss of me.*

The voice didn't respond.

"No, I mean it," the elf said.

Brightwing had almost forgotten she was there.

"One time a few months ago, Nima and I were walking around here and we *totally* saw someone from another village just fall right into the river! He got up and was all like 'oh erm—I didn't see you two.

I'll just be on my way,' and then he walked away. It was so funny. I mean, not that watching *you* fall in the river was funny. Okay, maybe it was. But it's fine, because you're not alone." The elf rambled on like a howler monkey.

"Okay, I get it," Brightwing snapped. "I wasn't paying attention, and now I'm wet. What do you want?"

The elf stopped and looked at him with curious eyes. "You know, I think I've heard of you. You were in the forest just a week or two ago, weren't you? At Lampis? The whole forest heard about you guys!"

"What?" Brightwing asked.

"Lampis, the village near the Skyspire!" the elf exclaimed. "You and two other griffins were there! News travels pretty fast here. I'm from Aqualin, the village a little south of here."

Brightwing tilted his head. "How many villages are there?"

"Three in the Silver forest," the elf answered. She counted on her fingers. "Lampis, Aqualin, and Synarn. But I'm sure there's more in other places, like at Clearwater Lake—I heard there's a really nice village there."

"Interesting," Brightwing said to himself. "I guess I just assumed Mira's village was the only one. Makes more sense that there would be more."

"I can't believe you're here again," the elf was saying. "Are the others with you? There was some rumor about you guys coming to find the spirits; did you ever find them?"

Get rid of her now, and it will be easier, the voice told him.

Brightwing froze. Did it just tell him to kill someone for no reason? Was this the same voice he had been listening to? So far it hadn't told him to do anything he regretted, and it even helped him on occasion. Like when they were at Quake Canyon; and he went to find another way into the cave Boreas and Dustbeak were trapped inside. The voice had led him to a tunnel that let him into the cave.

Then again, I guess Mira had already gotten in at that point. Could it have just been distracting me so I couldn't help?

"Hey, you don't look so good," the elf said suddenly.

Brightwing was torn out of his thoughts and looked up at her. She had hopped off her rock and was now standing at the edge of the water, fidgeting with the end of her shirt. Her eyebrows came together and she tilted her head, her eyes searching his.

"Like, really not good. Are you sick or something? Maybe you should get out of the water."

Brightwing didn't know what she was talking about. He felt fine. A little embarrassed and annoyed, but fine. He glanced down at his wet fur, which looked pretty matted. Maybe that's what the elf meant. He started wading towards land.

"Are you okay?" the elf asked, reaching her hand toward him as he neared the shore.

"I'm fine," Brightwing said. He heard a long, high-pitched ringing. "I must have just hit my head when I fell," he told himself.

"Your—your eyes..." the elf trailed off.

"What about them?" Brightwing glared at her and climbed up onto the riverbed.

"They—look in the river."

Brightwing turned around and looked into the water. He noticed nothing in his reflection at first, but as he watched the water something started to change. His eyes, which were usually a dark amber, were shifting and growing darker. He saw his golden feathers changing too, like a shadow was being cast over him. He glanced at the sky but there wasn't a cloud in sight.

"What in the world..." Brightwing murmured. He turned back to the elf.

"What's your name?" he asked.

"Una," the elf said carefully.

"Una, listen. Elves know lots of stories and myths, right? Do you know any that might be connected to this?" Brightwing asked.

The ringing in his ears was growing louder, and he had a bad feeling that this was more important than either of them realized.

Una frowned and thought for a few seconds, but shook her head.

"Okay. I need you to do me a favor. Can you do that?" Brightwing asked.

He was starting to feel cold, and the voice was whispering something to him that he couldn't understand. Over and over it repeated the words that meant nothing to him, but he was sure that whatever was happening had to be because of whatever was talking to him. And if it was blocking the sun spirit, it had to be something powerful.

He remembered the Shade from Quake Canyon, and how dark its eyes had been.

Una nodded and Brightwing continued. "If you ever run into an elf named Mira, I need you to tell her what happened. She's from the village by the Skyspire—Lampun or whatever it's called."

"Yeah, I know her. She's the dragon rider from Lampis," Una said.

"Okay. If you see her, you need to tell her what's happening to me. My name is Brightwing."

"Wait, where are you going? What's happening?" Una asked as Brightwing turned and spread his wings.

Stop fighting. Let it come. Let me in. All you have to do is relax.

Boreas held a talon to his head as the voice returned, stronger and louder than it had ever been before. It spat out multiple instructions, and Brightwing could hardly hear his own thoughts.

"I need to get out of here. Just go, before something happens," Brightwing said.

"But—"

"Go!"

Una bit her lip and nodded, starting to back away from Brightwing. His head started pounding with the voice screeching inside, and his ears could hear almost nothing but ringing. He jumped into the air and flapped his wings as hard as he could. He had to get away from here, away from everyone. He felt like he was past being able to save himself, and if that voice took over then no one would be safe. Maybe there was still some way to save everyone else.

Just let me in. There's no need to run. All your problems will be over soon.

Brightwing just flew faster. He couldn't let the voice win.

Suddenly there was a black frame around his vision. He ignored it and kept flying. *I just have to get as far away as I can.*

By the time he reached the edge of the forest, he could barely see. He couldn't hear a thing, and he could barely think. He saw a blurry image of the Silver Beaches as he soared over them. The ocean rolled beneath him and he looked straight ahead, towards the horizon.

Finally he couldn't handle it anymore. His head felt like a volcano ready to erupt. His eyes had given up completely and he could only see darkness. Every bone in his body felt encased in ice.

He just couldn't do it. He had to let the voice win. It was the only way to stop the pain.

He turned his head toward the sky. Though he couldn't see at all, he guessed it was long past sundown now because he couldn't feel any warmth from the sun. He had been flying for most of the day. He lowered himself closer to the ocean and felt the spray on his feet from huge waves. Maybe he was far enough from Arcenti to keep everyone safe.

Brightwing let out a deep breath and closed his eyes. The voice celebrated in long hissing whispers that Brightwing couldn't understand and didn't want to.

He felt all his pain stop at once, and his mind closed down. He let the darkness overwhelm him. The dark spirit had won this battle, but Brightwing was sure it wouldn't win the war.

Acknowledgements

Thank you to my parents, for always supporting me and inspiring me to follow my dreams. I love you so much and I hope I make you proud.

Thank you to Young Inklings, for giving me this amazing opportunity and helping me along the way.

Thank you to Melissa, for coaching me and helping me through this process. This book wouldn't be the same without you.

Thank you to the rest of my family for your support and love. I'm grateful for each and every one of you and love you so much.

Thank you to all the other authors out there for inspiring me.

And thank you to everyone who is reading this book. It has always been a dream of mine to become a published author and share my stories with others. I hope you enjoyed the book, and look out for more!

ABOUT THE AUTHOR

Faith Landfair is a 13-year old girl living in Arizona with her family and pets. She is in 8th grade and has five older siblings, all of whom she looks up to. When she was very young, she used to write stories in a small notebook she had. These short stories slowly evolved into writing full books. She began writing her first chapter book (which was never published) when she was ten years old, taking inspiration from the people around her and all her experiences. Aside from writing fantasy, Faith loves drawing, riding horses, and spending time with her family and friends. Her family is extremely supportive and she never would have made it without them. Apart from her parents and siblings, she also lives with a dog, a cat, and her guinea pig. Faith likes to take inspiration from her family and even bases some of her characters on them.

CPSIA information can be obtained
at www.ICGtesting.com
Printed in the USA
BVHW041343180422
634607BV00007B/134